Text Classics

HELEN HODGMAN was born Helen Willes in Aberdeen in 1945 and spent her childhood in Essex before her family emigrated to Tasmania in 1958 as part of the 'Bring out a Briton' campaign. After leaving school she worked as a bank teller, then as a teacher, and was involved in the Hobart art scene. She married the director Roger Hodgman and had a daughter.

In 1971 Hodgman left for London and wrote the first of her six novels, *Blue Skies*. Published by Duckworth in 1976, the scathing depiction of Tasmania in the late 1960s was lauded in major English and Scottish newspapers. *The Times* called it 'a joy to read'. Fans of Hodgman's writing included Auberon Waugh, Julian Barnes and Patrick White.

Jack and Jill, Hodgman's second novel, was published in 1978 and won the Somerset Maugham Award. Hodgman lived in Vancouver before returning to Australia in 1983, having been diagnosed with Parkinson's disease. She wrote for theatre, film and television.

The more experimental *Broken Words*, published a decade after *Jack and Jill*, won the Christina Stead Prize for Fiction in the New South Wales Premier's Literary Awards. Soon after, Virago published a bind-up of *Blue Skies* and *Jack and Jill* in its classics series.

Broken Words was followed by a trio of Sydney novels: *Passing Remarks* (1996), *Waiting for Matindi* (1998) and *The Bad Policeman* (2001). *Blue Skies* was republished by Text a decade later, with Eva Hornung, Carmel Bird, Nicholas Shakespeare and Peter Conrad among those praising the novel for its originality, caustic wit and striking prose.

Helen Hodgman lives in New South Wales.

DANIELLE WOOD is the author of *The Alphabet of Light and Dark* (winner of the *Australian*/Vogel and Dobbie awards), *Rosie Little's Cautionary Tales for Girls, Housewife Superstar: The Very Best of Marjorie Bligh* and *Mothers Grimm*. She is the co-author, with Heather Rose, of two Angelica Banks children's novels; the editor of *Marjorie Bligh's HOME: Hints On Managing Everything*; and the co-editor of *Deep South: Stories from Tasmania*. She lives in Hobart and works at the University of Tasmania.

ALSO BY HELEN HODGMAN

Jack and Jill
Broken Words
Passing Remarks
Waiting for Matindi
The Bad Policeman

Blue Skies
Helen Hodgman

Text Publishing Melbourne Australia

textclassics.com.au
textpublishing.com.au

The Text Publishing Company
Swann House
22 William Street
Melbourne Victoria 3000
Australia

First published by Gerald Duckworth & Co. 1976
Published by The Text Publishing Company 2011
This edition published 2017

Cover design by Text
Series design by W. H. Chong
Page design by Susan Miller
Typeset by J&M Typesetting

Printed and bound in Australia by Griffin Press, an accredited ISO/NZS 1401:2004 Environmental Management System printer

National Library of Australia Cataloguing-in-Publication entry
ISBN: 9781925498370 (paperback)
ISBN: 9781925410716 (ebook)
Creator: Hodgman, Helen, author.
Title: Blue skies / by Helen Hodgman ; introduced by Danielle Wood.
Series: Text classics.

CONTENTS

The Harsh Light of Day
by Danielle Wood

When I was seventeen, my grandfather bought me a plane ticket to London. For him, London not only had the strategic advantage of being far from the boyfriend I had at the time: it was also the most obvious destination for the cultural enlivenment of a girl born and raised in Hobart. I arrived there in early winter and, though I loved the city for its theatres and museums and crazy-angled street-corner buildings,

I was topographically adrift. The Thames was not so much a river as a concreted canal, and I missed my mountain. Worse, I felt myself pressed down upon by the heavy lid of sky that lightened later, darkened earlier and showed its blueness less often than even the very worst of the winter skies I'd lived beneath in Tasmania. I experienced several weeks of unbroken greyness before the clouds peeled away to reveal that, higher up, the sky was blue after all. Over-excited with relief, I took its photograph.

Back in Hobart, I had my photographs developed. I expected to have a blue rectangle, a slice of pure cobalt to commemorate the day the sky cleared in London. But my picture turned out to be pale blue at best, and unmistakably shot through with greyish tendrils of cloud. Perhaps my eyes played tricks on me, or my cheap pocket camera was never up to the task of capturing that sky, that day. Or perhaps blue skies are not as uncomplicated as they first seem.

✳

Helen Hodgman made the same journey in reverse. She was thirteen-year-old Helen Willes when she emigrated with her parents from Essex to Tasmania in 1958, as part of the 'Bring out a Briton' campaign launched by the Australian government. It was like stepping from black and white to colour. She remembers the sensory onslaught of the light, the vivid palette of nature and a perception that she had arrived in a world of greater social freedoms.

Social freedoms can be deceptive. Helen left Hobart High at fifteen and had a series of jobs, from a 'disastrous' stint at the Commonwealth Bank to waitressing, to working at a bookshop, where she finally started her education and met her future husband, Roger Hodgman. Their daughter, Meredith, was born in 1965. In 1969, Helen and a partner, Paul Schnieder, opened the Salamanca Place Gallery, the establishment that began the transformation of Hobart's signature row of historic waterfront warehouses into a hub for the arts.

In those years, in this place, Helen Hodgman was an observer twice removed. Not only was she from elsewhere: she was a writer, though yet to write a word, and she turned this twin X-ray vision on her surroundings. What she saw was a landscape of beauty and mystery, and the cracking veneer of an insecure, insular society desperately trying to make nice in the aftermath of the violent dispossession wrought by colonisation.

It took Helen's return to England, when she moved to London in 1971, for these technicolour impressions to find their way onto the page. *Blue Skies* took shape during six intense months in 1975. The title and its understated irony came early, born of her experience that a blue sky can oppress just as certainly as can a grey one.

It is common for Tasmanian literature to be soft-lit with the kinds of autumnal colours that are so flattering to sandstone convict ruins, a contrast to the red dust and white gums of much mainland Australian writing. Helen turns up the intensity, creating a glare under which she examines human desperation and ugliness. It is usual, in writing about Tasmania, for dawns and dusks to proliferate. Instead, Helen gives us broad daylight—precisely, a never-ending three o'clock. The unnamed heroine is, in this painfully deft portrait, suffering the crushing boredom and depression that can shadow the early days of motherhood. She is a curiously passive protagonist who is, as Helen describes it, 'very good at slipping sideways'. Fleeing the demands of her new baby, and the emptiness of her home and marriage, this young mother ricochets between the embraces of various and equally revolting lovers, flouting the social conventions of 'Tiny Town', all the while pursued by angry ghosts in the landscape.

The blue sky is a complex motif. Sometimes it is a perfect canvas in danger of being despoiled by the 'passionate reds and purples and boiling yellow-green jealousies' contained, just, within the abject human body. Other times it is a blazing firmament scorching the 'vulnerable, white bodies' that do not belong beneath it. In one startling pre-dawn scene the narrator even envisages the land as if from the sky itself, overseeing a tableau of the slaughter of Aborigines and seals, the fall of 'crimson drops on the golden sand'.

*

Blue Skies has many of the hallmarks of a first and youthful novel—confident and free-flowing imagery and dialogue, elements that appear to be semi-autobiographical, a risky ending. Like its narrator, the novel is sometimes abrasive and quirky, wilful and obsessive. But it had something that was immediately seen by editors at the venerable London publishing house Duckworth, that was also seen by contemporary critics and that will be seen by readers of this new edition: *Blue Skies* shines with raw, hard-edged talent. This book is—now, as it was when it first hit the shelves, in 1976—quite out of the ordinary.

English perceptions of the novel from the time of its release are both amusing and smug. The original Duckworth edition's blurb described Tasmania as a place 'where the sky is always blue and nothing ever happens', and I cannot help but smile at this, for I know how often it rains. London newspaper reviewers—nearly all positive—were almost too pleased to refer to Helen as a 'chronicler of awful Australia', to liken her command of the Australian idiom to that of Barry Humphries and the 'vulgarity' of one of her characters to that of Edna Everage.

The Duckworth edition of *Blue Skies* splashed the word 'incest' on the jacket, without consultation with the author, and even though the text contains only a hint of an over-involved brother and sister. When Virago republished *Blue Skies*, in 1989—packaging it with Helen's second novel, *Jack and Jill*—the new blurb continued to promise incest, along with the murder and suicide that the book does contain. Helen puts this down to the English being rather too interested in the notion of Tasmania as Australia's incest capital.

In the Hobart press, *Blue Skies* was warmly reviewed by the local literary matriarch Joan Woodberry, to whom the novel is dedicated, but other mentions of the book in the local daily, the *Mercury*, betray a dependable deference to the cultural standards of the Mother Country. 'A novel about Tasmania has recently been highly praised by London's hard to please literary critics,' boasted the newspaper in 1977. Then, in 1979, when Helen won England's prestigious Somerset Maugham Award for *Jack and Jill*, a *Mercury* headline made so bold as to claim her as a 'Tasmanian author', though she had left the state in 1971 and would never live here again.

Home, for Helen Hodgman, has been Essex, Hobart, London, Vancouver and Sydney. Her concise debut, the product of two of those places, is a blisteringly original contribution to Australian writing. Its bright colours undulled, *Blue Skies* remains a confronting snapshot of the social aridity of suburbia, the experience of marriage and motherhood, and life on the 'heart-shaped island' south of the mainland.

Blue Skies

For Joan Woodberry

At the bottom of Adventure Bay is a beautiful sandy beach... The other parts of the country adjoining the bay are quite hilly; and both those and the flat are an entire forest of very tall trees, rendered almost impassable by shrubs, brakes of fern, and fallen trees; except on the sides of some of the hills, where the trees are but thin, and a coarse grass is the interruption...In the afternoon, we were agreeably surprised, at the place where we were cutting wood, with a visit from some of the natives; eight men and a boy. They approached us from the woods, without betraying any marks of fear, or rather with the greatest confidence imaginable.

CAPTAIN COOK, WRITING OF HIS VISIT TO
VAN DIEMEN'S LAND, JANUARY 1777

At the last ball at Government House, Hobart Town, there appeared the last male aboriginal inhabitant of Tasmania... As savages they were found, as savages they lived, and as savages they perished! Such an event is deserving of some notice.

EXTRACT FROM THE SOCIAL NEWS,
MERCURY, OCTOBER 1864

I once had an aunt who went to Tasmania.

NOËL COWARD, *PRIVATE LIVES*, 1930

I'd watched it from the beginning.

Before she came, our house had been the last in the road: a tatty full stop to a long line of prosperous weatherboard bungalows. It stood out a bit, as it wasn't painted in a lurid pastel shade like the others—because I could never make up my mind what colour to do it. Dead colour-selection cards littered the house.

On the far side was a small patch of scrubby bush straggling to the beach, the one remaining unsold block. For days on end I could forget that I lived in a suburb just by looking out of the right windows.

Then the land was sold and cleared. Trenches were dug. Men built the house.

The woman who had bought the block came each day to the site to oversee them. I eavesdropped behind my blinds as she whined at them to get on. The large sun-reddened men were unmoved. They took their time, pausing at regular intervals to brew billy tea, smoke and grin shyly at her through large mouthfuls of meat pie.

The work was quickly finished, and the house balanced on an uneven area of raw reddish earth. The men left. It was a wet time and afterwards rainwater stood round it in slick, sky-reflecting puddles. The sun glinted and flashed on those pools, surrounding the house with a fence of reflected metallic shards.

The woman hired another gang of large soft men, who levelled the earth and drained it. They dug it and primed it to receive the sackfuls of domesticated grass seeds.

These the woman tended herself. A square of spiky grass blades stood before the house, a vivid and unreal green. Impressive at a distance, but close to it looked pretty sad. The blades were far apart. The dusty earth, growing dustier as summer passed, showed through the gaps like mange and defied her daily watering.

The native grasses rustled and swayed at the edge of this pampered patch. Occasionally it would stake its aboriginal claim to the usurped homeland by launching a seed to fertilise and reclaim a centimetre. Tough though it was, it could not take the almost daily shaving.

*

In those first few lawn-laying days the woman would be at the house early in the morning supervising the seeds. She seemed in no hurry to move in, as she waited for the grass to grow. I would pass her as I walked back from the beach, but she was too absorbed to speak, keeping herself to herself, which was good while it lasted. If she introduced herself, the beach spell would be broken. With luck and no interruptions, it would work for me all day. The beach was the main reason for my living there.

I had found it during a weekend visit to my future in-laws. My pregnancy having been confirmed only twenty-four hours before, there was no hurry, I thought. But my husband liked to do things properly. The problem was to break the news and find somewhere to live.

I had gone for an early morning walk to ponder these things and came upon the beach, over a slight rise in the road at a point where it looked to go on forever but merged at the bottom of the slope into a stretch of cutting coarse seagrass, ending at the beach in a tangle of car tracks which petered out into the sand.

Surprised early in the morning, it was a marvellous beach—a holiday-brochure cover of a beach. On each side it stretched away, pale yellow and perfect. Startling black rocks jutted up in contrast at either end, the sea bluest blue with silver-lamé glitters. It was an absurd extravagance of beauty so early in the day, a whirl of colours that I associated with midnight hours. I sat down in the dust among the empty beer cans and wept.

I was stranded up on that beach like the poor dumb female turtle I once saw in a film. It had just laid a load of eggs in great distress and difficulty and hadn't a hope of making it back to the sea, but, exhausted, was going to die.

Walking back up the road I saw a house for sale.

We borrowed money, bought it and moved in. My husband worked hard; he needed to repay the loan and prepare for his financial fatherhood. I sat back like the turtle and waited to die.

It didn't happen. The days passed and I began to doubt it would—numberless days when the clock always said three in the afternoon, no matter what you did to it. You could try turning it upside down. You could try catching it out, peeking suddenly round the door and taking it by surprise. No matter what you tried, the day ran out then, and there was nothing left to fill it with.

All the other women in that nature reserve for

females managed to invent something to fill their time in decorative and reassuring ways suggested by the women's magazines—those placebos prescribed to sugar-coat time and keep half the population quiet and useful. But such schemes required spirit, an urge to fill days acceptably. I had none.

*

The beach waited in its early morning perfection just for me and the odd dog-exerciser. When the sun rose higher, the pale yellow sand became an almost desert blaze. The black rocks crouched like primitive worship stones, antipodean Stonehenges.

Later, when the noon blaze subsided, the local women came down. Those nearest would walk laden with bright beach bags and babies, carting the many necessities for enjoying an hour in the open. Those from further up the road would drive, the wheels of their small economical second cars spurting up dust sprays and rutting the sand at the edge. Most people gathered together towards the ends of the beach. The hitherto mysterious rocks were then pressed into domestic service, their flat tops used as tables, their crevices as storage spaces for cold drinks and for keeping bits of clothing out of the sand.

As older children escaped from school they joined their families on the beach. The sand was dug up and shaped into castles, giant initials, holes through to China. The murmurings of mothers and sun-stoned babies were overpowered by shrill competitive shrieks, the sounds of unwinding that followed release from school. Mothers and babies gathered their things together and left. There were evening meals to be cooked for returning husbands, sprinklers to be switched on, clothes to be taken down from the rotary hoists standing in back yards—suburbia's garlanded totems. The older children lingered on, following their own patterns, guarding their freedom until their mothers' warning cries arose in the dusk and drove them back indoors.

My boredom grew up in the midst of plenty—plenty of people. I even had one right inside me: it kicked from time to time to remind me of its presence. Built-in company.

But you don't think of it like that, or do you? I put the point to my gynaecologist.

'Do you?' Oh God, he was handsome, especially when he smiled.

He smiled.

'Well, no. That is an unusual way of putting it. I find that most women see no further than the unquestionably important business of getting the baby born. The future is hidden from them as if by a curtain.'

'Or a venetian blind,' I suggested, thinking the answer didn't go with the question.

'If you like.' Another smile, but his heart wasn't in it this time, you could tell.

✳

The baby was born just in time for me to spend my first day home from the hospital watching the new neighbour finally move in. I parted the blinds and peeped out, wondering, with the rest of the street, at the width of her television screen, the simulated-leather dimensions of her three-piece suite, her cocktail cabinet, her funny-looking lawnmower.

Next morning she spoke to me. There was no avoiding her. She was out of the house, dragging the mower behind her, and had me bailed up before I could move.

'Gooday,' she said. 'I'm your new neighbour. Olive's the name, but call me Ollie. Always start as you mean to go on, that's what I say.'

I said I was pleased to meet her.

'Mutual, I'm sure. Lived here long, have you? I'm a stranger in these parts myself. I've come over from the mainland to give it a go in Tassie. Been here before on holidays, of course, me and my late husband. That's when we got the idea.'

She was polishing the lawnmower, unwinding a long flex which she plugged in just inside her sunshine-yellow front door. The machine howled into action, hauling her across the grass in its wake.

She shrilled back at me over her shoulder. 'Isn't this a little beaut? Bet you've never seen one of these before, have you?'

She was right. The electric lawnmower had yet to make its mark on the Apple Isle. She finished her demonstration with a flourishing figure-of-eight round my feet and switched off.

'Not bad, eh?'

I agreed. Secretly I thought it dangerous. I wasn't the only one. People were always leaning over the fence and handing out advice. I did so myself on the bad days when any diversion would do.

She assured us all—her well-meaning neigh-bours—that she knew the dangers: 'Youse have just got to be very careful to see that nothing is on the grass, like a stone or twig or something. It could fly up into the machinery and make an electric shock.' So before she started she always combed the pathetic patch of sun-scorched stubble with a rake she kept just for the purpose.

She mowed the lawn several times a week, and it didn't get a chance to grow. From the time she spent on it, I think she was probably as bored as I was. Maybe we could have discussed it and filled our time taking flower-arranging courses or something.

Instead I stayed behind my dusty blinds, occasionally parting two plastic slats to watch her work.

'It's the same the whole world over,' I crooned, watching my breath cloud the window glass and wondering if it really was.

My neighbour, who had more sense, toiled mercilessly on. I concluded that for her it was an obsession: a contest with nature, an epic struggle or something of the sort.

*

In the weeks that followed I felt it my duty to take my daughter out each day for an airing. We went down to the beach to join our peers. I listened carefully while my fellow mothers talked of this and that. The baby wriggled in her wicker basket, protected from the sun by the useful shadow of a rock. I joined in where I could, politely voicing carefully considered comments rehearsed in advance. The conversational topics were raised in a circular way, one for each weekday as it came round in its turn. Mostly I eavesdropped and felt superior as they chattered of knitting patterns and incest: scarcely a day passed without talk of some hopelessly deranged mutant being found chained to the wall with the family dog outside some inland shack, an irredeemable mess of genes—and all because its parents didn't get about much. Back in town, the Country Women's Association Choral Society was preparing for the fiftieth annual Gilbert and Sullivan Festival.

The image in my mind of the poor stranded turtle was replaced by one of a seal colony, the mothers and the babies huddled together in steaming heaps on the beach, father away providing.

When the seal imagery wore thin I conjured up another. The hopeful, shiny pumpkin face of King Kong appeared on that line between sea and sky. Enormous arms stretched towards us from the horizon, hairy hands across the sea. King Kong picked up the women between thumb and forefinger, gathering them in the palm of his hand. The hand sank back into the sea, holding them in a gently bubbling bouquet beneath the waves. Only I remained, alone on the beach. When the bubbles subsided he let them go, and they sank gracefully, turning long watery somersaults down to the sea bed. His pumpkin face shone down on me; his wrinkled leather slits of eyes twinkled happily;

his fist closed about my waist. He raised me up, penetrating me with his pointy hairy little finger until I disappeared into the clouds, borne heavenwards on a rising chorus of cries from the abandoned babies.

I stopped going to the beach.

I concentrated my efforts not on airing the baby but on abandoning it. By being polite and behaving well, I could buy myself bits of free time. The person I had mostly to be nice to was my husband's mother. This was because she lived at pram-pushable distance and loved looking after the baby. Not every day: that wouldn't have been right. But she was good for two days a week.

Tuesdays and Thursdays. On these days I could take off and forget the street, the beach and three o'clock in the afternoon.

I chose not to forget my neighbour. Her obsession interested me. I made up stories about her, so that my friends would also be interested. Between us we built up quite a saga around Our Lady of the Lawn.

I had two friends. One for each day. Both men. Finding accessible men during the day was difficult. It seemed that proper men worked nine-to-five, with a gap of an hour in the middle, and you can't do much in an hour. At least I can't.

Ben was a painter, but he also did photographs

and drawings. He was for Thursday, saving best for last. He was married to Gloria, my oldest friend.

The necessity for a bit of pulse-racing secrecy did a lot for me. Ben became exciting. He made a nice change. I remembered Gloria's own excitement when she first met him. It was in the park near the art school he attended and the teacher's college where she was training. She had been sitting on a bench eating her packed lunch, and Ben had come along and sat down at the other end. Noticing his hungry look and empty tucker box, she had offered him one of her landlady's home-made sponge fingers.

'He's different,' she told me. 'He's got this flat in one of those houses behind the college. His bedroom is lined with silver foil like a tea chest.' Gloria had all the luck in those days.

Jonathan was Tuesday. He managed a restaurant—which those who knew about such things thought the best on the island. I had worked as a waitress there, nights and weekends. We became friendly the day Jonathan took me to one side and let me in on a secret. 'Listen,' he said. 'Everyone can see through your dress when you stand in front of the light. It's transparent,' he added, faintly unnecessarily.

'I know,' I said.

'Oh well, that's all right then.' He looked relieved

to hear it.

We took to drinking together after hours in the empty bar. The bar was the best thing about the place. The restaurant lacked atmosphere—candles in bottles or no candles in bottles. But the bar was nice. It had a marble top and bottle-filled glass shelves fixed high on the wall behind it.

Next to the bar was an enormous black refrigerator, the first I had seen, in which ice and cold drinks were kept. I admired this exotic refrigerator, even though it showed fingermarks terribly; few people could resist touching it lightly with their fingertips as they passed. You could just see your face in it, if you looked hard enough.

The next best thing about the restaurant was that it was underground. Once down the stairs from the street you were safe. As you sat in the bar, with its dim light and many dull shining surfaces, time passed quickly and unnoticed.

Jonathan went with the restaurant, as much a fixture as the black refrigerator. He had come to Australia to spend his old age—as he was fond of saying—in the sun. He was moon-faced and pale, and rarely seen above ground in daylight; his grey hair grew in marcel waves down past his collar: he didn't blend with natural surroundings. Small boys would follow him down the street chanting 'What d'yer use on it then, mate—Curly Pet?' and he would hurry away from them on his out-turned feet, his pursed mouth and mincing walk laying him open to charges of 'pouffery', the Australian crime against the sanctity of mateship.

Jonathan claimed to be an ex-British Army Captain and had a repertoire of adventures. From the background of these tales it seemed he had lived through the Indian Mutiny, but nobody took him up on the details, because they were good stories.

He claimed friendship with the beautiful people who lived overseas, a hard claim to disprove because so few turned up in Tiny Town. Those who did appear, usually in some professional endeavour aimed at entertaining the locals in return for their money, always came to his restaurant. When they turned up to feed, Jonathan was pleased. He drew a chair to their table and recommended dishes, and this often annoyed the cook, who had other menus planned. Undeterred, he would scurry off to the kitchen and prepare the food himself, causing confusion and resentment among his kitchen staff. He would often ponder the causes of his high staff turnover, putting it down to the aggressive streak he detected in all his new countrymen. To support his efforts he always gave the visitors free bottles of a wine he kept for just such occasions. Like all the wines he served, it was Australian. He considered this one special, and seemed to imply to any eavesdropping natives that it was surprising that an Australian wine should be so good.

This made him something of a marked man, but he remained unaware of that.

On these occasions he could never resist joining the party: he would sit quiet and content for a time, basking in the reflected glory and the conversation, which was a cut above what he usually suffered.

Sooner or later he would start to bloom like some forward, pale-faced flower. He would take over the conversation. Mainly by telling jokes. Funny jokes. All types of jokes—finally downright repetitious and boring jokes.

Enchantment faded. Moves were made to be getting on, pleasant though it had all been, pleased though they were to make his acquaintance, and they would certainly recommend the place to all their friends. These moves would be blocked by offers of one more bottle, more cheese, more coffee, more anything. This was usually late at night. The absence of staff may have deterred the guests from taking up his generous offers.

In the long gaps of time between the visits of these romantic strangers, he had to make do with the local crowd. They flocked in in droves. They were not as glamorous, it is true, but they were reliable, especially the lunch-time lot, who consisted mostly of local celebrities—some exciting television comperes from the two Hobart stations, some journalists, one of whom was said once to have written for mainland dailies.

A separate group was made up of the local arts-and-crafts men, who comprised a large part of the local population. In the long summer days, if the wind was in the right direction, the sounds of potters potting and weavers weaving rose to a disturbing crescendo. At night, unable to sleep, I would try to calm myself by lying still and counting relentless rows of pleasant little greyish-brown mugs and other bits of improving pottery jumping over fences.

It was Jonathan who diagnosed the complaint that we both suffered from, and I was surprised at what he had to say. Drunk or not at the time, he showed me a remarkable contrast to his usually insensitive exterior. There he stood, revealed and psychologically naked in that greasy neon-lit kitchen, his fingers stuck deep in a glass bowl of prawn cocktail. We were hiding in the kitchen, afraid to go outside because we feared that a drunk rugby team was waiting to bash us up. Jonathan said that if they didn't clear off soon he was going to call the police. Meanwhile we waited, eating up everything that wasn't likely to last through till Monday.

'You know, old girl,' he said, 'the trouble is that I am so piss-awful scared of people. They terrify me, especially when they gang together in groups. I suspect you feel the same way.'

I didn't say so. Obviously a whole bar-full of over-excited athletes, convinced that he was homosexual and determined to put him right with a thumping, had unsettled his nerve.

'I don't just mean that lot upstairs,' he went on. 'They're much too obvious a manifestation of the syndrome. The really frightening ones are the people who cluster together in the so-called better type of suburb. The golf club joiners, those who keep other people out, who want them in their proper place in this so-called classless society, who like to have a good laugh at anything unusual, who are terrified of anything new and different—the worshippers of the great pepper-grinder god. I'm not putting it well. Never mind. Forget it. Silly to talk like this.'

It wasn't that silly. I thought of the women on the beach. I felt the same way. Perhaps I was scared of them— it seemed better to be scared than to be stuck up.

Before I left Jonathan's employ in a premature panic at finding myself pregnant, it was arranged that we should stay friends. Tuesday seemed a good day for it. I would go up to town and see him on Tuesdays.

Usually we would have lunch at his own corner table near the kitchen, so that he could go in there and fuss through the busy times without too much inconvenience. Lunch was always exciting; and I always drank a lot, and talked too much; he rarely listened.

Afterwards, after locking up, I would go back with him to his flat. While he slept in preparation for the night's excitements, I roamed around playing his records and tapes and soaking up the atmosphere. He was the first person I knew who had headphones, which were a bit unnecessary since his flat was above a warehouse.

※

The pink-and-grey vinyl radiogram with gold knobs that my parents gave me for my seventeenth birthday was never the same again, and I put it in the carport, along with other unwanted items. The carport slowly filled up with rubbish. Wedding presents went in first and on top of them piles of newspapers, magazines and worn-out obscene publications smuggled in from foreign parts; broken things that may have been mendable; large amounts of just plain garbage that I was ashamed to put out for our irate garbage-disposal men who grudgingly crawled round once a week at 2 a.m. or thereabouts. They wouldn't take cartons of rubbish, only two neat deodorised plastic garbage cans per house.

I fretted over where people put their excess rubbish. Surely they must have some. Probably a great deal went onto compost heaps and incinerators in back gardens, but both seemed mysterious and faintly dangerous to me. So all that shameful excess went into the garage. After a while I gave up packing it in cartons, and just opened the door enough to get my arm round to hurl the old tin cans and bottles inside as far as I could.

After some months of this I noticed, to my horror, that the double doors were beginning to bulge outwards. Terrified of exposure, I piled bricks in front and tried to forget all about it. On the hot days I thought I could detect a faint but sickly smell, and local dogs took to sniffing round the doors and moaning ecstatically. I became nervous and imagined germs and rats breeding out there: I saw the rats pouring forth in a seething stream to bite the sun-brown babies in their prams.

In the pink pages I found a refuse-disposal firm. They agreed to come and solve my problem, even though I wasn't an industrial unit—more a health hazard. Two men worked all day with shovels removing layer after layer. The further down they went, the more compacted and unpleasant it became. As I sneaked an occasional look, it seemed to me like the geological layers that are exposed in a cliff by erosion: thousands of years squashed into a one-inch stratum. Finally they scraped the remains of the wedding presents up from the concrete floor and drove the lot away in a truck. The pink-and-grey vinyl-finish radiogram with gold-plated knobs and luminous station-finder dial lay on the floor beside the driver. I was glad it had found a good home. For twenty dollars I had bought peace of mind and a sense of virtue. I just hoped nobody would find out.

✳

I might have saved myself some embarrassment if I'd had them call on a Thursday. Thursdays I was out. Thursdays always started bright, and they always started early. Bright and early, there I'd be, pushing the pram up the road, round the corner and down the next road but one.

✳

The pram squeaked, and my brain squeaked along with it, keeping time. It squeaked with the effort of wondering what to say to Mother-in-law waiting round the next bend. You couldn't just dump a baby and run. She wasn't that kind of person.

The truth is, I didn't talk much to anybody. But Mother-in-law I did talk to. There she would be, in bed in her lovingly crocheted pink bed-jacket, preparing for a standard Thursday-morning chat.

Her bedroom was at the front of the house; large windows faced the street, draped and discreet for no purpose. There were pink-painted peeling French windows at the side, opening onto a gloomy concrete verandah. This in turn led down by some steps at the opposite end, onto the front lawn. The lawn was badly drained and boggy—a very imperfect lawn. I thought of bringing my demented neighbour round to look at it, by way of reassurance.

Down the street we would go, shattering the early morning daze, making little puffs of dust as we kept carefully to the sides of the road. Safety first. Dust rose to settle all over the teak-veneer coffee tables in all the houses down the road. The sunny hum of early morning hoovers filled our ears.

A big daring swerve took us to the middle of the road, ready for the big run-up needed to carry us over the swampy lawn without getting stuck. We bumped backwards up the steps, front pram wheels spinning noisily in mid air. A final hearty shove across the concrete verandah and we were at the peeling pink doors. They were open.

'Good morning, dear.' There she was, sitting up in bed, surrounded by litter and all the props of a poor sleeper, sipping milkless, sugarless tea from a thermos flask. I crossed the room and sat on the bed.

'Good morning.'

'How is James? He said he would call in to see me on his way home last night, but he didn't. I expect he'll telephone me today. Or call in this evening.'

James is her son: the youngest, the nearest to home, the one I'm married to. James hadn't come home last night.

'Oh he's fine. But tired, you know. He's really busy at the moment. I'm sure he'll phone today.'

'Well, my dear, you mustn't let him work too hard.'

Here followed various health warnings and gloomy predictions as to what might happen if James worked too hard.

Next, Angelica. Angelica is James's daughter, the baby, and her grand-daughter. 'How is Angelica? Oh, do bring her in. I long to see her.'

An Angelica-sized space was cleared and she was carried in from the pram and placed face down on the bed. It may not look natural, but face down was how she liked to be: she got into the habit at the hospital where she was born; they programmed her to do it from birth. 'It brings up the wind and is comfortable for Baby,' they said. Not only that. At the moment it showed off her plastic pants to best advantage. They had an extravagant rosette on the seat, made up of different-coloured ruffs of pastel plastic. I had bought them the day before at the Baby Bar in the local chemist. I awaited delighted reactions complacently.

'Oh, how sweet. Oh, aren't they fun. You do look after her so beautifully, my dear. I will say that.'

Terrible vistas opened up of what she wouldn't say. We both have this problem of what to call each other. She has settled for 'My Dear'. I have settled for nothing.

'Do go through and make yourself some coffee, if you want. There should be some nice biscuits in the tin.'

I went—there was still a quarter of an hour before the bus to town passed the top of the road, and I was starving. The coffee made, biscuit tin placed under one arm, I returned to the bedroom.

'My dear. Couldn't you find a plate? I'm sure you could if you looked.'

There wasn't much time left now. The rest of the conversation was obscured by the biscuit cramming my mouth. It kept getting stuck and the coffee wouldn't make it go down.

'You'd better go. You'll miss your bus. I'd hate you to do that on my account.'

'Goodbye.'

I kissed her cheek as she expected, and patted the baby on its plastic rosette.

'I'll try not to be late.'

'Don't worry, my dear. You know how I love to have her all to myself. You cut along now and enjoy yourself.'

I cut, and quickly. My left sandal strap snapped as I ran up the street to the main road. Just in time: I could see the bus approaching at high speed. It pulled up; the pneumatic doors folded back. I climbed up the steps, paid the driver, and fell into the nearest seat. I wound down the window and threw the other sandal out. Barefoot and free. You couldn't pile it on too thick on Thursdays.

*

From town I took another bus, a country-bound bus, square and slow. Full of mailbags and chicken crates, it went out through the surrounding bush townships in the early morning and came back in the late evening. The driver was young and greasy. I thought he must be English. He wore his hair in a beautifully oiled duck's tail; it must have left dreadful marks on his pillow or wherever he kept his head. He wore a purple suit and blue suede shoes. A large Japanese transistor radio balanced on top of his dashboard. It crashed against the windscreen at every hole in the road and was never quite on the station, but gave a pleasant blurred effect with occasional blasts of static. That bus had atmosphere. Today it also had a team of lady bowlers, who were off to an away match at a country ground. They were arranged two-by-two along one side of the bus, exchanging pleasantries and egg sandwiches, their starched white dresses and uniform hats giving off static of their own. Their bright enamel club badges glittered and flashed victoriously in the sun; their stringy brown calves rippled healthily above sterile white socks. The bus had a clinical air this morning; in contrast the driver looked dirtier than ever. The newspapers and loaves of sliced white bread in their waxy red-and-white wrappings were loaded into the back.

We moved off, creaky and overloaded, crawling through the suburbs to where the thin stream of weatherboard houses trickled out into a pool of rusting car bodies, rotting mattresses and ragged-edged beer cans. The telegraph poles continued, pulling themselves out of the tangled mess of the town into a taut straight line and marching purposefully ahead from horizon to horizon, ignoring geography and natural obstacles and playing tricks with perspective.

First off were the lady bowlers. They disembarked just past the airport and disappeared into a little wooden clubhouse by the roadside. We drove on, round scrubby hills, blue-green and smooth at a distance, coarse-grassed and rocky up close. Dotted on these hills were little trees with rounded tops: toffee-apple trees from nursery wallpaper. Overhead the high bright blue sky was stretched tight and shiny between pink-tinged clouds. The road ahead was a shoelace of white dust. The colours were primary, hard-edged, acrylic-clear. I scraped myself, in my bus shell, across the perfect clarity and colour of that day—a bag of white skin full of passionate reds and purples and boiling yellow-green jealousies. If the bag split, those colours would spill out and spoil the scenery. But it didn't. There was no bursting with happiness. Or anything else.

As the bus lurched round the next corner I saw Ben waiting. He was waiting for his mail, he said. He had a lot of friends overseas, and their pale blue letters filled his canvas mailbag and his life with interest.

Once Ben had tried living overseas. He took his wife and son and went by boat to England: to a small dingy room in London, where the rat aspects and dirt of big-city life got him down. So they moved to a small provincial city in the Midlands, where they rented the last house in a long row of grey terraced houses. Some claimed that it was the longest terrace in England; later the National Trust put a preservation order on it. The end house, his house, ended in a blind brick wall facing bleak countryside. During the first week there he borrowed a ladder and painted his wall with a bright tropical landscape, and it became a local landmark. A man from the *Sunday Times* came and took a photograph of it, and it was reproduced in the colour supplement as an example of urban street art. Someone cut it out and sent it to him, and he pinned it on his workroom wall. It hung there now, fly-spotted and brittle-yellow with summer heat.

Through his back windows Ben had been able to see nothing but ploughed fields, in which, it seemed, nothing was ever planted or grew. In winter, snow fell and it was white and silent all round for miles—except for his incongruously glowing tropical landscape. It was so glittering and pure and clean that his nerve broke. One evening, after picking a quarrel and breaking all the windows, he ran away, back to London, where he spent ten grey days, worrying his wife sick as she waited it out in that cold English landscape burning his pictures to keep his son alive and warm. So he had nothing to show for it. A wasted trip.

I knew of this, not from him, but from Gloria. We sat together one day by a dried-up summer creek; she with a shoebox of photographs to show me: mementoes of the trip. To make the most of it, they had taken the long way home, through Europe and various other bits of the world. She showed me a photograph of herself with son in arms on top of the Leaning Tower of Pisa.

'That's where I had decided to commit suicide. I was going to jump—I would have put the boy down first, of course—but Ben stopped me. I think people who try to stop other people killing themselves are boring. And stupid.'

She placed the lid back on the shoebox and told me the story of their trip. Her face in shadow under her large sun hat, all the snow and ice and the miserable solitude that she described seemed safely at a distance— a vast distance. I smiled and held her hand as we walked slowly back to the house. I hoped that she felt safe in her hot land.

I saw Ben waiting for the bus, the mail and, it being Thursday, me. The bus pulled up at his feet. The dancing dust surrounded him in a cloud. He was wearing a long black djebella and sandals—a misplaced Arab.

The local people thought him mad.

They thought his wife noble, fine and long-suffering.

They thought his son a poor little mite to have such a father.

In the town, among the more sophisticated who could think of these things, it was rumoured that he took drugs.

It was rumoured that he slept with his sister.

Stories were told of how, at the age of thirteen, he had run away. He went missing one midnight and stayed so for weeks, while his frantic parents had the entire state police force out after him. When he was found in the central highlands sitting in a clearing stark-naked chewing roots, they took him away and talked to him on couches, and gave him electric shocks. It had done no good, it seemed. So much, they said, for modern medicine.

Crazy Coot.

They bought his pictures, these town folk. Slowly at first, but as his exploits became more embroidered, the more his pictures sold: a bit of decoration to hang on the wall; a bit of himself; a bit of scandal; a conversation piece.

Today his wife had left in her battered blue station wagon to teach at the local school. She took their son, who was in the infants' class. She worked to support the painter, while the painter dreamed of success in the posh private galleries of the mainland, where people are prepared to pay more, being used to that kind of thing.

But these are all my conclusions. He did not speak of these things to me, but let me dream around them. Sometimes this annoyed him, and sometimes I thought it amused him, but he let it happen either way. I found myself telling stories about him, and I told them to anyone who would listen. I tried to stop it, but could not help it. He said nothing. I knew he knew what I was doing: spinning my life out of his.

✳

I got off the bus, and Ben collected his mail. We went to the house, an old colonial farmhouse, beautiful and battered. There was a great deal of land attached to it, but Ben didn't farm the property. It belonged to his sister, and he let bits of it to a neighbouring farmer to graze sheep, while the other bits he left to nature. A creek ran roughly through the middle. In summer it was a canyon with steep, hard, red-earth sides and a few slimy puddles at the bottom; in rainy seasons it flooded. He had channelled some of this creek water into a pond, where he kept ducks for his own amusement.

We walked around the house to the back door, which led across a small wooden porch straight into the kitchen. There we made tea, and then we sat at the large pine table and rolled cigarettes and smoked them, gazing thoughtfully into each other's eyes. We wondered why I had come.

'So,' he said. 'Good morning. Let's go.'

We went through to the bedroom. It contained twin beds. Once I had taken this to be a sign—a bad marriage: all was not right in the bedroom—where all the problems start, my mother said. But this time my mother and I were wrong. He told me how it was.

'When you sleep together you naturally cuddle up, right? Nice and cosy. Mmmmmm. Why not? Well, what happens is, it drains you off. All that touching gets to blunt the edges. So you don't want to fuck so much. Right?'

'Right.' He was making speeches. Leaving clues for me to go over later.

'This way is better. You go to bed together for one reason. When you really want to. It's good. Very sharp. You have the best times when you feel like that.'

'Really?'

'Yes, really. You should try it. Or maybe you wouldn't like it. Too straightforward for you. You're too bloody evasive. So *soft*.' He said it like a long word, smiling all the way through. 'Soft at the edges, but hard as rocks somewhere in there. Very nasty.'

'Put your glasses on,' he said, 'and get what you fancy out of the trunk. A bit of old velvet might be nice.' He went to his bed and pulled it out from the wall into the middle of the room. I took my clothes off. It was terribly hot in there. The windows, blistered shut in some past heat, wouldn't open. Ben climbed over his bed and disappeared. His head reappeared on the far side and spoke. 'There's some new stuff we can try today. A beaut little number I picked up in the Salvation Army shop in North Hobart.' He vanished again.

I went over to the old trunk in the corner of the room and searched through it for something interesting.

This trunk was Gloria's pride and joy, her family heirloom, which she seemed to love out of all proportion. It was only a load of old clothes after all. Once upon a time, she told me, it had contained some bits of old cranberry glass, a Bible and the family silver, as well as old clothes. Gloria's mother had disposed of the valuables years ago, but Gloria didn't care: she liked the clothes best. She was fond of describing their romantic history: how her great-grandmother had lugged the trunk out from the old country long ago, in the days of sail, packed full of her best things and lengths of silk, velvet, lace and several pairs of little white gloves which the old lady had supposed it would be hard to lay hands on in the Antipodes.

Gloria regularly dosed the trunk with mothballs and lamented the damage done by silverfish. Ben and I started playing with this stuff one day, a few dressing-up games that just lately had got a bit out of hand. Ben had developed what I considered sometimes to be an unhealthy interest in old clothes.

'Here, try these on,' instructed Ben from behind his bed. His latest purchases rose into the air, somer-saulted over the bed and crumpled in heaps at my feet.

Ben stood up and dusted himself down. He shoved his bed back against the wall to cover the loose floorboards. He kept his bundles of second-hand clothes in plastic sacks in the space between the floor-boards and the foundations: his dressing-up clothes, the stuff of fantasy, chosen for their colour, their texture, the way they felt on the skin.

Gathering up armfuls, we went into his work-room, a glassed-in verandah along two sides of the house. We made a soft, shifting, multi-coloured mountain in the middle of the room.

Alone with the heap of beautiful things in the silence—the silence that comes from being enclosed in thick sunlight. It insulated us like thick golden cotton-wool. It kept out air; it kept out sound. It kept us isolated and secret. It was too thick to penetrate the glass; it wrapped itself round the house. We were playing in a private golden ball.

We played with our pretty mountain. We chose the pieces of material and clothing we needed. We needed them to act charades—the Victorian parlour-game kind: choose a word, act each syllable and then do the whole word. We took it in turns: one-man shows. Sometimes it was very funny, and we laughed a lot. Sometimes it was very sad, and we made ourselves cry. Occasionally we would be drawn into frightened fantasies. He would twist my arms, give me Chinese burns, whip me with his plastic belt bought in New York, rub me between the legs with his choicest materials, take polaroids of my reactions, stride about in Chelsea Cobbler cowboy boots—Kings Road souvenirs—masturbate into a faded pink velour Victorian remnant. Colourful times. Hot days. We ended asleep, buried in clothes drifts.

Ben woke first; made tea; held the steaming mug under my nose; brought me round with chocolate biscuits. He said I slept like a dead fly—on my back with arms and legs sticking skywards. There were a lot of dead flies in the workroom. They rimmed the window ledges in dry black lines. When a breeze disturbed them they rustled like leftover Christmas decorations.

❋

Packed away, washed, dressed, brushed and fully restored to order, we sat sipping tea and chatting till his wife and son returned. Since we didn't have much to discuss, we spoke mainly of my neighbour. I reported to him our brief conversations, which he considered cryptic.

Ben wanted to meet my neighbour. I had told him that this wasn't possible, that she'd die of shock at the sight of him, especially wearing a dress. Ben looked pleased at this. 'How about,' he suggested, 'I drive down and park outside her house. I could just watch her and she'd think I was a travelling salesman taking a break.' But I didn't trust him. I saw him leaping from the car in a frenzy and doing dreadful things on her lawn—the kinds of things I'd heard vandals did on altar steps in churches. Half of me found the prospect delightful, but the day-to-day half decided it couldn't cope with all that outrage. I kept putting him off.

When conversation lapsed I looked at his pictures. There were always several in various stages of completion, and piles of drawings. One large painting he was working on was of my head—a very large head, with narrowed watchful eyes behind the cracked pink sunglasses I usually wore, surrounded by riotous scenes of naked men, women, children and animals enjoying themselves in most possible ways. All this joyful activity went on under my cold, once-removed and possibly critical gaze. I recognised little scenes taken from our dressing-up days. And in a bottom corner, very small, a middle-aged woman mowed her lawn.

By the time our mutual boredom reached its pitch, his dependents returned. Gloria and I left father and son together and took off for the hotel in the nearest township, bouncing over the impossible little roads in a cloud of dust, swerving to avoid the worst potholes.

'Jogging up and down in the little red wagon,' she sang happily. 'Jolting up and down in this rusty blue wagon,' she laughed, one hand on the steering wheel, the other swatting wildly at some gaudy, dangerous-looking flying insect that had been sucked into the car.

I trailed my hand out of the window, the air buoyant as water.

'How was school?' I asked politely, to get something going.

'It was all right. Same as usual. Don't let's talk about that. How's your tiny nuclear family?'

'It's all right. Same as usual. Don't let's talk about that.'

*

Gloria didn't know James very well. She had been overseas during our brief haphazard courtship, and the letter I had written to her about it, care of Tasmania House in the Strand, she claimed not to have received. I had described it since: how we kept bumping into each other at parties and rebounding off into the night together for long talks. James had been the first man to explain the American electoral system clearly to me. One pretty evening, as we sat side by side on the end of a falling-down wooden jetty in the moonlight, he asked me what I had been doing when Kennedy was assassinated. For one wild moment I thought he was accusing *me*. He went on to say that he thought it would be one of those things that, whenever it was mentioned, people would be able to remember exactly what they had been doing at the time.

'Like the day war broke out,' I agreed. 'My mother told me she gave three cheers the day war broke out, because she had this plan to lie about her age and run away from home to join the Land Army. '

James looked puzzled but wouldn't be put off. He really wanted to know what I had been doing at the time. I said I couldn't remember, so I supposed I was asleep. I was relieved that this undramatic information did not put him off. James was very interested in America.

In the course of our talks I conceived a dreadful passion for him which I went to ridiculous lengths to assuage. He finally obliged me one night on the back seat of his mother's car in the back row of the drive-in movies where a lot of that went on. *Alfie* was showing at the time. Michael Caine flickered wanly across the screen suspended in the sky while James struggled wildly to free his feet which were entangled in the speaker wire. In the end he solved the problem by booting the speaker out of the car, where the actor's adenoidal tones squawked away unheeded on the gravel. We only just got sorted out in time to be sitting respectably upright when the floodlights came on. Car doors slammed all round us as people rushed from their cars to the refreshment area underneath the screen. James nervously flicked his hair from his eyes and adjusted his clothing. Taking my hand, he carefully explained the situation to me, so that there should be no misunderstandings later. He had a lot of girlfriends, it seemed—filter-tipped secretaries from work whom he took to Saturday-evening dinner dances at local motels. He bought them steaks at the Starline Grill, which revolved while you ate, with panoramic views of the wharves and the gothic mountain that loomed behind the town. These girls didn't go in for drive-ins and that kind of thing, he implied.

When I found that I was pregnant and he took me home to meet his mother, it was like winning a lottery you didn't know you had tickets in. You don't know whether to laugh or cry.

✳

So Gloria and I wouldn't talk about that. Instead we kept our minds on higher things.

'Those gum trees,' I said, meaning the gum trees that lined the road, their trunks patched and stringy-looking, but graceful and pale at the same time, 'are just like Greek columns. Like bits of a leftover civilisation.'

'No they're not,' she said. 'I bet you've never seen any real Greek columns.'

She knew that I hadn't.

'The sky,' I ventured, 'is a beautiful blue. If a little unnatural.'

'Well, you do know where you are with a beautiful sky of an unnatural blue. It's those moody grey skies that keep naturalistically changing that I don't like.'

We sang 'My Blue Heaven' in harmony all the way to the hotel—well, the chorus, anyway.

In the bar it was very exciting, because we were not supposed to be there. Not that there is a law or anything, not any more. We just weren't supposed to be there—females. It caused a lot of nudging and desert-boot shuffling in the bar. It caused painful moderations of the spoken word—a distortion of comradely language—which we liked. We liked the jukebox too. One song we would play over and over. I hoarded five-cent pieces all week for that purpose. Tammy Wynette would hit shrill notes—*Stand by your man*—while we rocked back and forth with the kind of giggles you can't stop at the time but should grow out of.

We always drank brandy and dry ginger—you don't need so much of it. We would buy a bottle and drink there, and take the rest back—plus a bottle of wine that the barman would dig out of a room at the back with the air of one discovering buried treasure.

The rides back were better than the rides there. Stops were made to admire rocky shadows, ghostly gums, the moon, the stars and the Southern Cross— but where it was I never discovered for certain; fortunately it's on the flag. The conversation was not so good—more and more a question of semantics. Pick a word and elaborate. More and more that word would be jealousy. After various definitions made on various rides back from the hotel, I came up with a winner.

'Why,' I said brightly. 'My dear, I do declare, I do believe it's the only thing that makes your life worth living. All that excitement keeps you going.'

'Maybe that's right,' was what she said.

*

When we got back she started to cry, quite quietly— then loudly and a lot, all over her dinner.

'What have you been saying?' Ben muttered at me. 'What's happening? What's the matter?'

She left the table and fled bedroomwards: door shut, lock turned, dull Bette Davis sobbing. Meanwhile back at the table all was Joan Crawford stifled hysteria and grimacing.

'What did you say to her?'

Since I couldn't tell him what it was, or whether

47

it had to do with me at all, I couldn't answer. He bent my little finger back, hard. But nothing came to mind. So that was that.

✳

This was not the usual Thursday evening behaviour. It spoilt the Thursday pattern and was the first of the signs that Thursdays were ending. It proved to be the penultimate Thursday. I blame myself.

Usually Thursday evenings were much nicer: good food accompanied by lots to drink, and faint surprise that alcohol worked as well as anything else—and let you talk at the same time.

'I can't get off on words,' Ben would say. 'Pictures are more my thing.'

Somewhere out there in the dark, the bus was always getting closer. Usually I tottered down to the gate and stood swaying as it pulled up. I could just make it up the steps and into the front seat.

If I wasn't already hovering mothlike in the head-lights, the driver would honk his horn and hang about till I appeared, which was nice of him. Perhaps he was lonely. Not once was there anyone else on the bus for the Thursday night trip back to town—just a lot of objects: bags of potatoes and pumpkins, boxes of eggs, leftover newspapers, mail sacks, things like that. I wondered whether he was lonely on other nights, or whether each night he had a different lone passenger.

I used the homeward journey to sober up. He used it to make conversation. He told me once how, in his youth, he had been a big number-one Eddie Cochran fan. 'You know Eddie Cochran?'

'I've heard of him,' I said, humming through a few bars of 'Summertime Blues' to be nice.

'Yeah, well, you're maybe a bit young,' he said kindly. 'He was killed. Went out on his motorbike. The best way there is. All over the road. He was the greatest, no question.'

'Like James Dean,' I said, anxious to please.

'No, he was a film star. It's not the same thing. An American film star. Jesus Christ.'

For a while he drove on in disgusted silence, making the bus hit all the ruts and ridges in the road, to teach me a lesson. Something dark, furry and forgotten scuttled along the bus, in the shadow of the seats.

Then he resumed our chat.

'For five whole years after Eddie bought it, me and the other real fans used to hire a charabanc and go to the place where he died and put flowers on the road. We'd have a motorcycle escort out in front. In black leather gear like Eddie wore. Those were the days, like they say. The good old days is right. It's all changed now. The whole country's gone down a lot. No sense of direction. To think, we used to lead the world.' He sighed regretfully, squashing a headlight-dazzled possum under the nearside front wheel. 'That's why I've come out here. It's the country of the future, no question.'

'Oh, for sure.'

*

On the night of the sad domestic drama, he unexpectedly ground to a stop with a crash of gears and a scream of static from his transistor. He switched it off. Eerie night noises started up in the bush.

'How about it then?'

'What?'

'How about it then?'

'How about what then?'

'How about that then? You know.' He gestured with his greasy head towards the long back seat of the bus, leering prettily. 'No one ever comes along here, this time of night. Or I could pull off the road behind them trees, if you'd rather.'

I don't remember it clearly. A lot of free-range eggs didn't make it to the breakfast table that morning.

I was covered with chicken feathers, egg yolk and news-print when I got back to town. I tried to get some of it off in the taxi going home. I didn't attempt the news-print—most of it was it was in places that didn't show.

I always took a taxi home from the rank opposite the GPO, it being too late for a bus. I left the cab at the top of the road and tiptoed down to collect Angelica. I could never tiptoe enough, though. The voice usually sprang out of the darkness just as my cautious toes left the top step and my anxious fingers curled round the fly-screen door. The bloody thing squeaked.

'Did you have a good day, my dear?'

'Yes, thank you. Did you? Was she good?'

'Oh, of course she was good, the little darling. We had a lovely time. We went to the beach this afternoon. I do so love to show the pretty little thing off.'

'Oh good. I'm glad everything was all right.'

'James came round. Well, he was hungry and I expect the poor boy was a bit lonely. He had dinner here with me and we watched television together—I did enjoy that. He left a couple of hours ago. He must be wondering what's happened to you, my dear.'

'He does it on purpose,' I confided to the baby as we trailed homewards. She slept peacefully on, as did her father until we reached home. He awoke the second the fly-screen door squeaked.

'Like mother, like son,' I told the baby. She smiled sweetly in her sleep. I wheeled her into her room and left her in the pram rather than risk waking her by lifting her out into her bassinet. As soon as the motion of the pram stopped she whimpered. I flipped her over on to her tummy, kissed the furry back of her head and turned to do my tiptoeing act out of the room. Daddy stood smiling sleepily in the doorway. He looked fuzzy at the edges, dark brown with sleep.

'I've got to oil that bloody fly-wire door,' he said. 'Remind me. I'll try and do it tomorrow. Might as well go round and do Mum's at the same time. Have a go at that bloody pram too, while I'm at it.'

'Good idea,' I said. 'Why didn't you bring Angelica back with you from your mother's tonight?'

'Well, I knew you'd be going there anyway. You weren't expecting me to collect her, were you? Although you know I would, don't you? I don't mind. Any time. You've only got to ask.'

He stepped aside so that I could pass by him out of Angelica's room. He was big and soft, with lots of shiny dark brown hair. His eyes and mouth filled his face; both were much too big for aesthetic balance.

He seemed fascinated by something on the floor. 'Your feet are filthy,' he murmured.

I took a shower. And so to bed.

When James was back asleep I unravelled myself and got up. The chance to go forth babyless to the beach was too good to miss. Husband, wife and child asleep under one roof seemed one person too many: security goes in twos.

Approaching the rise in the road I saw that the sky behind it had a peculiar back-lit orange quality, like the setting for some show that was about to start. It was the dawn, and I reached the beach in time to see it. I tried to ignore it. Dawns are too theatrical for me, and this one looked particularly stage-managed, with every conceivable overdone effect. After the sun had squeezed its way out of the invisible slit between the sea and sky, the water flushed momentarily red, as if covered with a slick of afterbirth. Later, when it settled down, the light was violet-coloured, and the sea and sky glowed gently like the inside of an oyster shell when wet. The air was clean and fresh, like your mouth after toothpaste. A new start.

Someone had put up a swing. It stood there at the top of the scraggy-grassed slope to the beach, with its dark institutional-green tubular iron frame, bright new chains and plain wooden seat. It was a well-made and official-looking swing, clearly the work of the local authority. I stared at it. Small pains started in my head, one behind each ear: anger and guilt. 'Take my eyes off you for one day,' I screamed at the beach, 'and look what happens.' My voice shrilled high and horrible, running along in both directions and bouncing back off the end rocks in stereophonic fury. The sound met in the middle of my head, and the pain overwhelmed me. I had to sit down, and so I sat on the swing. Back it went, then forward, a seductive swing. My toes, reverting instinctively to childhood, kicked hard into the dust and met the ground at just the right place in the swing's backward arc to make it swing the more. The seat warmed against my skin. I pulled up my skirt and snuggled my bottom against the smooth grainy wood, wrapping my hand in the chains and hanging by the wrists in a rush of air. I closed my eyes; my head fell back. I recognised the signs. Swing rape. Desperate to get away I tore my wrists free and jumped. My knees were grazed, my legs cut by the coarse grass. My wrists were scraped and bruised from the chains. They hurt badly as circulation returned, and blood formed little bead bracelets round my ankles, where the grass had wrapped and cut. Sitting down in the dust, propped up against one iron leg of the swing, I watched as each little blood bead grew until it became too distended to contain itself. One by one the beads overflowed and trickled down, tiny red ribbons round a maypole. I picked up a sharp-edged stone, which looked useful—a tool: a long-dead Aboriginal hunter's weapon. I jabbed its sharp point into the swing's leg, but nothing happened. The paint was too thick, all its molecules bound tightly together, impervious and permanent. I turned my weapon on its side, and scraped down hard on the paint. A curl of colour came onto the stone. I scraped down hard again. A thin layer of the swing's paint skin clung onto my stone. Again and again I scraped down, my teeth grinding with effort. Layer on layer of paint came away. The paint on my stone was thicker than the paint on the swing. The steel bone lay exposed—just a small piece. I rubbed the exposed area with my finger. It glittered faintly. The sunlight was getting stronger. Tiny flecks of green paint clung on my sweaty fingers. I picked each green morsel off with the point of my tongue, and it tasted bitter and dangerous. Lead poisoning. I recalled sad old newspaper tales of dead infants still and cold in their playpens, mouths smeared with colour from lead-painted toys, and I tried to spit it out, but couldn't. Paint is persistent: it does its job and clings to surfaces to which it is applied. Why worry? I had just decided to have a go at another leg of the swing when a dog barked close by. A man and dog walked along the shore, and I straightened up from my kneeling position beside the swing. My legs were a streaky mess of blood, sweat and dust. Man and dog turned and came towards me up the beach. I shielded the wounded swing with my body. My fingers closed around the stone.

'Are you all right, miss?' His first words of the day, they seemed, rumbling up from his sleep-stilled stomach. 'Has there been an accident?' He blinked around the deserted, still misty, horizon, as if looking for a possible cause. Under my astonished gaze the mists rolled back, revealing an entire invasion fleet of warships, with guns pointed at the defenceless shore. Just as quickly they vanished. The scene played on. I suddenly felt very tired.

'No, not really. I fell off the swing. Silly thing to do. I never could resist a swing.' I tried convincing him with a matching silly-girl smile. My face was too tired to make the effort. I glared at him instead. He glared back and walked on.

I put the stone in my pocket and walked down to the water. The sand was starting to warm; individual gritty crystals glinted slyly between my toes. I walked into the sea up to my knees, and the cold saltiness of it stung antiseptically in all the tiny weals and cuts. I scooped it up it against my face until I became calm and composed. Time to go home. Lines of glistening white shells edged the shoreline in a frothy lace cuff. I picked up a handful and put them in my pocket with the stone. The sand felt hotter under my sea-chilled feet as I walked up the beach; the day was beginning. The dog ran back towards me, a shaggy black cannonball which swelled as it got closer and rushed past me and up the slope to the swing. Skidding to a stop, it lifted its leg and pissed all over my handiwork. At least the dog had noticed.

I walked home. It was slightly later than I supposed. The paperboy raced down the street on his bike, hurling newspapers at all the front doors. He was a good shot: rolled-up parcels ricocheted in all directions thumping onto the wood verandahs, landing in dust clouds in the parched front gardens. Seeing me approaching, he threw a paper at my head, the greatest fast bowler around.

'Gooday Missus. Up early, aintcha?' For some reason he winked suggestively. Gripping his bucking bike between his brown bony knees, he prepared to throw my neighbour's newspaper onto her front lawn. Its mangy back seemed to quiver in anticipation of the assault. As it hit, a few blades of defeated grass lost their grip on the earth, flew upwards, fell back to earth and died, and a soft collective sigh of wounded grass filled my ears. I waited till the boy had gone. The street was still again. My neighbour's venetian blinds remained tight shut. Inside the house she slept on, dreaming perhaps of pampered croquet pitches, well-kept golfing greens and camomile lawns in a world without water restrictions. I took the shells from my pocket and threw them over the miniature ranch-style fence.

*

Angelica still slept through a great deal of the day. That day I would do the same, avoiding the horrors of three-in-the-afternoon and the flatness that sometimes came with Friday.

James was in the kitchen perched on a stool at what was described in the furniture catalogues as a breakfast bar. It had a white formica top with silver flecks in it.

James was not eating breakfast. He was propped on his stool in a dream, swaying and drooping slightly like a parched flower, his head hanging limp. His hair brushed the white and silver surface, and I saw that he was reading a book. He looked tired and pale—a little unglued.

'The phone's been ringing. It's been ringing since Christ knows when. It woke me up. It was scarcely light first time.' He groaned and rubbed his eyes. They seemed to smear all over his face.

'Who was it?' I asked. Breathless ladies in pay-phones were forever ringing him up. It made me cross, because I always wished it was for me.

'How should I know? Each time I said hello, whoever it was rang off. I took the bloody receiver off in the end. Then I couldn't get back to sleep, so I gave it up.'

'Why didn't you stay in bed and read? It would be more comfortable surely?' I felt guilty. Sure the calls had been for me.

'Oh, the bed's in such a bloody mess I couldn't be bothered to make it just to get back in. Let's see the *Mercury*.'

I gave it him, walked through to the sitting room and put my stone into the blue-and-white pot on the mantelpiece. I replaced the phone and sat on the floor and waited. It didn't ring. The sun poured through the slats of the blinds in self-contained streams, which spread on the carpet in puddles. I curled up in one of them, pressing my cheek into the hot prickle of carpet pile, nearly asleep. From the kitchen came the sound of water filling the kettle. There was a clank as it hit the stove—a scrape of match and a rush of flame: James making tea. More sounds, each separate and distinct, crossed vast spaces to reach my ears: James making toast. James stood over me, his toes level with my eyes. I bit the largest toe in reach.

'Look out, I'll drop this lot on top of you if you're not careful.'

I rolled over and sat up. James was carrying a tray of tea and toast, the toast already buttered and cut into tidy triangles. We sat on the floor in adjoining sun puddles and ate. I held my face in the scented steam rising from my mug of tea and felt the little beads of sweat pop out. The phone went on not ringing.

James licked his fingers and spoke. 'I'd better go. Want to get an early start. I'll try not to be too late tonight. I want to fix those doors. Then we'll borrow Mum's car and go up to the supermarket.'

Late-night shopping Fridays. I would have to make a list. I couldn't face that huge supermarket without a list: it was a map that got you round and out the other side safely. James preferred to be adrift, lured off course by colourful outcrops of special offers, following red-lettered signs that led like siren songs to neatly stacked islands of stuff we didn't need. We always spent too much. I worried about the money, and I worried more about getting rid of the plastic bottles, empty tins and excess packaging.

James was on his way out. 'Bye, love.' Squeak; bang and gone. Off into the real world. In her world,

Angelica was waking up. I could hear her rustling about, snuffling and grunting sweetly. In my world I was feeling threatened by non-disposable rubbish and the phone's not ringing. In her world Angelica's sweet temper was beaten back by feelings of hunger and wetness. She bellowed.

The morning went in sequence. Changed and fed Angelica. Bathed Angelica in a yellow plastic bath on the white-formica-with-silver-flecks breakfast bar. Carried Angelica to her pram, a neat little pink package carefully wrapped and pinned to keep the contents in. Sparse mouse hair escaped from one end, puffy cross red feet from the other. Changed the pram mattress cover and placed Angelica face upwards on it. Fastened coloured row of square- and circle-shaped plastic rattles threaded on elastic from one side of the pram to the other. Fixed sun umbrella onto the hood. Wheeled pram with Angelica in it round to the side of the house under the bedroom window where a young tree lent a crazy paving of shade. Spread fine net, like a veil, over the pram to keep off flies and things. Went back into the house. Heard Angelica gurgling and kicking the rattles, catching at them with her toes. Filled the automatic machine with dirty clothes including the ones I was wearing. Set it on its cycle. Went to bed. Went to sleep.

The phone was ringing. I was coming up towards a bright light, surfacing in a series of quick dreams full of unsuccessful attempts to stop bells ringing. I rolled off the bed and started in the right direction, colliding sharply with the edge of the door as I went. The pain of a stubbed toe joined the bells in my head and forced me to concentrate. Then the bells stopped. The phone had stopped ringing and I hadn't made it; with more sleep I might have done.

It was very hot in the house. The sun seemed to be baking directly down on the corrugated iron roof. It was probably lunchtime. As yet Angelica showed no signs of stirring. I went through to the kitchen to make coffee, put the kettle on and took James's place at the breakfast bar. The paper was lying open at the *Mercury's* double spread of social notes and recipes. My eyes reeled over the fat thick black print and small photographs of people with rigor mortis and inky skin blemishes. Under one, the caption read: 'Mrs Barber chose a long frock of floral chiffon mounted over blue which featured long flared sleeves with a rouleau bow over the midriff.'

'Rouleau bow' had a nice round quality to it. I turned the phrase over in my mouth, sounding the two words like a soothing spell, as I tipped all that remained of a jar of instant coffee into a cup, piled in the sugar and poured the boiling water on it. I found an end of pencil by the sink and sat back on the stool. I started my shopping list on the margin of the recipes page.

Large jar inst. coffee
2lbs sugar

I wrote this next to a headline which said:

BRIOCHE WITH A TANG
Here's a brioche with a difference! An intriguing filling of marzipan is rolled into a dough…

The phone was ringing.

'Yes, hello,' I said.

Someone was being strangled on the end of the line.

I said the number.

'Hello, old thing, where have you been? I've been trying to get you for hours.'

A familiar voice. Only it seemed to be strained through a barbed-wire sieve.

'Why, what's the matter?'

There was a constant background noise. A plate smashed somewhere, cutlery rattled. I was right about it being around lunchtime. I thought the restaurant must be unusually full to make that amount of noise.

'Haven't you seen the paper, old girl?' He sounded rather offended.

'Yes. I mean, no. I haven't read it properly yet. Why what's in it? Something to do with you? Fame at last?'

'I can't tell you. Go and read page three.'

'All right.' I put the receiver quietly down by the phone and went back into the kitchen, sat down and turned to page three. I read it.

I didn't hurry back to the phone. I sat and finished my coffee slowly, and read it again. It took a long time, although it was only four half-columns of words. I went back to the phone, hoping he had hung up, and put the receiver against my ear. He hadn't. The background noise seemed to have intensified, a sound that mixed anger and excitement; blowflies made the same sound betraying the presence of corpses. It was not convivial. Outside, I dimly heard Angelica start to cry. I heard Jonathan breathing through the phone, loud and close in my ear. He was waiting.

'I've read it. I don't know what to say. Why are you there?'

'I couldn't think what to do. I've been up all night. I couldn't stay in the flat. I thought of coming down to your place.'

'You can't do that.' He knew that I didn't say this because of what I had just read. Nobody came down to the house during the day. Nobody saw me playing a role I didn't choose.

'What will you do?'

'I don't know. It's bad here. I was mad to come and now I can't get out. There are people outside both doors and I can't face getting by them.'

'You could call the police. They'll have to protect you, clear the people away.'

'No. I can't face the police again. It's not protection I need, anyway. Everyone thinks it's bloody funny. They've just come to laugh at me.' His voice started to quaver—the strangling noise again. Outside Angelica was roaring.

'Look I'm sorry but I have to go. The baby's crying, you see.' I waved the receiver in the direction of the noise, hoping he would hear it and not think I was lying. 'Anyway, you must be doing a roaring trade. All publicity is good publicity, isn't that what they say?' I laughed sympathetically—to show I was joking. Silence. I waited for him to say goodbye or something. I feared for Angelica, crying so much out in the heat. If she dehydrated and turned to dust, would they blame me? Angry, I hung onto the phone, trying to stop him without having to feel guilt-ridden afterwards.

I was still looking for words when he said: 'Half the staff didn't turn up today. Including the barman. He phoned up to say he was sick. The others didn't bother with excuses. Bruce is in the kitchen, but there's no way he can cope. You couldn't come up this evening and give him a hand, I suppose?'

'No, it's hopeless. I can't get away. I'm sorry.' Outside Angelica was mewling and hiccuping desperately. A car was coming down the road. I knew the engine note: my mother-in-law's car. It stopped outside. The door opened and shut, and footsteps hurried towards Angelica as if drawn by a magnet. The choked crying stopped; cooing noises ensued. Child and grandmother slammed into the house. Two heads stared round the door at me. Angelica, far from having dehydrated, had apparently blown up, as if filled with soggy air. Her puce tomato face bobbled at me over her grandmother's shoulder. Her eyes had disappeared in swollen pulpy flesh, her lips quivered sadly across her face like reproachful purple slugs, her arms waved in the air like floating saveloys. It was the sort of thing you felt tempted to crush, but wouldn't, for fear of the mess it would make.

'So there's a naughty Mummy, then, gossiping on the phone.' She was waving Angelica at me, holding her up so that somehow the words seemed to come out of Angelica's tummy like a pre-recorded message. I turned my back on them both.

He was still going on. With the inflection of someone ending a long debate he said '...so I suppose I'll just have to close for a while if I can't get more staff.'

'Yes. Well, why don't you? At least until the fuss dies down. It will all be forgotten in a week or so, you'll see.'

'Maybe. But it will all start up again when it comes to court. I might have to close up for good. Or sell up and begin again somewhere else. On the mainland.' He sounded doubtful. 'That's if I'm not in prison.'

I hadn't thought of that. 'Oh, surely not. How could they? It's ridiculous. I'd be surprised if the police even have a case. The whole thing will probably be chucked out of court.'

'No. You don't understand what this is all about. The police have been after me for a long time, you know. I'm not well liked in this town. I know too many things about too many important people. Certain people would be very glad to see the back of me.'

Embarrassed by this paranoia, I said: 'Yes. Well,

maybe. Look, I really have to go now. James's mother is here. I have to talk to her—make her a cup of tea or something boring like that. You know how it is. Phone me again, won't you. Any time. Let me know what's happening—if there's anything I can do. I'll come to the flat on Tuesday, OK? Will you be there?'

'I don't know. I may go away somewhere. Trouble is, I can't leave the state because of the bail. Can't you come up to town before then? I mean, if I could just get a little help and keep the business going I could possibly face this thing down. I just need a bit of moral support, that's all. Then I can make these bastards pay for the privilege of staring at me.'

'Listen, I'm really sorry about this, but I can't come up to town before Tuesday. Tuesday's the day James's mother looks after Angelica. It's difficult otherwise. I can't lug her up to town with me.'

'No, I suppose not. Perhaps I'll phone you over the weekend. If I'm in town on Tuesday we'll meet somewhere. Thanks for talking to me. Goodbye.' He hung up on me.

Well, I hoped I'd helped get the whole thing into perspective, that's all. It was nothing really, a storm in a teacup. It had its funny side too, although you couldn't expect him to see that, I thought, following the sounds made by Grandmama and Angelica. It would all blow

68

over; there was no real point in my going up to town to help. Tuesday was soon enough. By that time we would probably be able to sit down and laugh about it together, which would be fun. I wasn't going to be put off being his friend by a bit of scandal.

Grandmama and Angelica were in the bathroom. Angelica was being washed out in the hand basin. The water had shrunk her back to her usual perfectly balanced and pale proportions. A neatly folded pile of baby clothes lay ready for her.

I leaned in the doorway. They were too absorbed in each other to notice. I went into the kitchen. Angelica was just starting on solid foods. I studied the neat rows of tinned baby food in the cupboard and took out one of minced brains with carrot and one of banana custard. I was just heating up the brains when they came in.

'Would you like to have some lunch with us?' I asked politely. 'I'll just feed Angelica, then make us some sandwiches or something. I should have some food somewhere. We're a bit low at the moment. The end of the week and all that. James was hoping to borrow the car this evening so we could go up to the supermarket.'

'No thank you, my dear. I'm not hungry. I don't eat much you know; it's not good for you in this heat. I only came round to see if I could borrow Angelica for the afternoon. I've got an old friend coming down and she's just dying to see my only grand-daughter. It's just as well I came when I did. The poor little thing was in such a state.'

'Yes. Well, Jonathan Pickup was on the phone and I couldn't stop him talking. I couldn't just hang up on him. I mean, I really couldn't think what to do.'

'Well, that's up to you of course, my dear.' She rolled her eyes at the paper open at page three. 'If I were you of course...' She didn't finish, but stared up at the ceiling as if seeing visions and said: 'Such a sordid little man. One always knew of course that there was some-thing not quite right about him.'

I served Angelica's steaming brains into her bunny-rabbit bowl. Taking her from her grandmother, I sat on a stool with her wedged more or less upright on my lap and started to spoon the colourless goo into her mouth. Too late I realised I had forgotten a bib. I fielded the thin rivulets of rejected food that ran from the corners of Angelica's mouth as best I could. This took so much concentration that I barely heard James's mother wondering aloud on the comparative merits of convenience foods and foods pureed lovingly all morning by caring mothers. Angelica didn't want it anyway. I didn't attempt the banana custard. It was a relief for both of us when the time came to finish off with her bottle. I put a little more formula in to make up for her not having eaten much. Angelica's whole body quivered in anticipation as the rubber teat hovered above her mouth.

Her grandmother sat on the other stool and watched this happy domestic scene with satisfaction. Afterwards I did my best to sponge the stray brain spots from Angelica's pretty yellow smock. She was going visiting. I helped load her on to the back seat of the car. She chortled up at the vinyl roof from the wicker depths of her carry-cot. Her grandmother leaned towards me over the passenger seat and spoke to me out of the car window.

'Why don't you phone James and tell him to pick up the car on the way home from work? I'll keep Angelica round there until late tonight. Then you can get your shopping done in peace.'

'Oh, that's lovely. Thank you so much.' I smiled with genuinely surprised gratitude and waved goodbye enthusiastically.

A high cracked voice seemed to come out of the air: 'She dotes on that little baby, can't you just seeyut?'

I hadn't seen her there, standing dead-centre on her pride and joy.

'Must be nice for her, having you all so close by.' She laughed as though she had just made a joke. 'Tell you what. Just step over here a minute. Got something to show you.'

I stepped over the miniature ranch-style fence and walked delicately over the grass towards her. She dug into the pocket of the stiff brown smock thing she wore while tending her lawn. She waved an agitated clenched fist full of something in my face.

'What is it?'

She unfolded the fist close up under my nose. It took me some seconds to focus on what it was. My shells.

'Found them, I did. Early today. Chucked down on me lawn. What a thing to do. I ask you. Some kids I suppose. Makes me mad, I must say. You work and slave to make the place look decent and then some drongos come and pull a stunt like this. They coulduv done some damage, you know. Got sharp edges, these things. Coulduv got trodden in. Damaged the roots. Lucky for them they didn't, or they'd have had me after them pretty quick, I can tell you. Come to think about it, I'll bet it was that paperboy that did it. He'd better watch out for himself, that's all.'

I looked sympathetic. 'Oh well. No harm done, I suppose.'

'No. Suppose not. Still, it's not right, is it? I mean to say. It's an uphill battle as it is. What with the poor

72

soil and all them old tree roots I couldn't shift up out of it. Now people are chucking litter on it.'

'Why don't you put covers on it at night like they do on cricket pitches?' I suggested: it was about the same size. I said goodbye and went inside. Looking through the sitting-room blinds, I saw her thinking it over—pacing it out and making notes.

I washed up the bits of used crockery dotted round the house. I hung the washing on the rotary clothes hoist out at the back, noting as I did so the subliminal whine of the electric lawnmower drifting round from the front, and phoned James. He wasn't there—wasn't in this afternoon, be back later, someone thought he had said. I left my message, found all the remaining food in the house and stuffed it between two slices of faintly stale bread, and took it to bed with a book. The book and the sandwich lasted the same length of time and then I was asleep, at first half-thinking, half-dreaming about phoning Jonathan back and finding out how things were going; but then sleep was deepening all around and I couldn't. James was there, standing in half-dark by the bed. I recognised his knees. The waist of his trousers appeared to be below them. He seemed to be undressing. Thinking very slowly but logically, I moved across the bed. He wriggled in and lay facing me.

'Hey, sorry. I didn't mean to wake you. It just seemed such a good idea. You looked nice curled up in here. You feel nice too. Except for the crumbs.'

'What's the time? Did you get my message? We'd better get up. I haven't made a shopping list. What are you doing?'

'It doesn't matter about the time. Yes, I got your message. Which is why I came home early. We don't need a list, and you know what I'm doing. I'll do it some more. That's if you don't mind.' James was a gentleman. It was a result of his perfect upbringing.

Rising to these high standards, we showed each other quantities of style and finesse over the next hour or two. It might have been the result of good breeding, but most likely it was practice. It set the mood of the weekend, which passed quickly and well. We made the supermarket just in time and so avoided lingering and arguments. Afterwards we had dinner at an Italian restaurant in a new suburban shopping arcade. It had red-and-white check tablecloths and a black-and-white tiled floor and candles, and smelled of paint and pasta.

✳

We managed rather well in our role of happy young marrieds and sustained it through Saturday and into

Sunday. On Saturday I thought often of phoning Jonathan and seeing how things were. I even thought of going up on Saturday night and helping out, as James was at home. But I did neither.

On Sunday night thoughts of phoning him nagged harder. James was asleep, the house quiet: there was nothing to prevent me. But remnants of the weekend mood kept me in another dimension, suspended above my own action. As I sat at the large pine table in the living room I tried to conjure up Ben and Gloria. But they came to me only as blurred and faded shades. Usually they flitted somewhere in my head accessible to my thoughts, a subconscious shadow-play which sent bubbles of action without detail up into my mind, but now they wouldn't come into focus. I sat at the table. It was very quiet. From time to time the old fridge in the kitchen rumbled and shook, the only sound. The blinds were up and the moonlight was just strong enough to see by without extra light. I played patience, a game of Japanese Rug with four packs of cards. The cards were placed alternately straight and sideways in a multi-coloured quilt. I got three games out from five played and went to bed while still ahead.

*

Monday morning. James was shaving. Cleaning his teeth. Getting papers together. Polishing his boots. He walked to the door, where he paused and fixed his let's-be-grown-up-about-this face on. Turning, he showed it to me and said:

'Look. I just don't know when I'll be home. If it's tonight it will be late, so don't expect me and don't wait up. You know how it is. I can't help it—got so much work on just now.' He excused himself through the door, which squeaked appreciatively after him. Another squeak: his head came back round the door and spoke again.

'Sorry. I'll fix that bloody door, soon as I get a chance. See you later. Take care.'

So I took care all day long. No point, I thought, in phoning Jonathan now. I'd be seeing him tomorrow. If he needed anything he would call me anyhow. He knew I'd do what I could to help. I looked forward to our lunch together. With luck he'd have his sense of humour back—have got things more in proportion.

✳

That evening I laid out my going-up-to-town clothes, choosing them with care and anticipation. Next morning, as early as I dared, I put them on, and after the usual trip round to the next road to deposit Angelica, sat in them on the bus composing opening lines in my head. I got off the bus at the square with the fountain in it and walked quickly to Jonathan's flat, climbing the wood-and-iron stairs at the side of the warehouse and knocking on the large brown painted door. There was no answer. I called out.

'Hi Jonathan. It's me. Can I come in?'

No answer. I pushed at the door, and it opened: it was on the latch. I went in. Obviously Jonathan had gone out for a minute and had left it open for me. Inside I crossed straight over to the record shelves to choose something to play. The shelves were empty, the stereo deck gone. Looking round the walls, I saw that the best pictures were gone too, their empty frames leaning against the walls. There were also gaps in the bookshelves.

I went into the bedroom. All seemed normal. I opened the wardrobe. There were clothes hanging there, but again there were gaps. I returned to the living room and sat at the table, feeling sick and frightened. Tuesdays had done a bunk. What should I do? I sat staring down at the floor. At my feet were little splashes of blood, dried brown and powdery at the edges, still red and sticky at the centre and making a neat trail to the door. I started to cry—because he had left here bleeding, because I had lost a friend, because I couldn't think what to do with the rest of my free day.

I went back into the bedroom and lay down on the bed to cry properly. The beautiful fur rug was gone. There was a crumpled newspaper on the bed: a weekly paper, a tabloid printed on the mainland, Australia's biggest-selling scandal sheet, which was always good for a superior laugh. 'Wife-swapping circle uncovered in respectable suburb.' This story, written in a polished style of shocked journalese, ran in neat black lines beside a photograph of a naked girl straddling some rocks on a beach. There was a front-page story of great local interest. Jonathan's face looked out, in a slightly younger version, from a maze of smudged print. There were other photographs: the outside of the restaurant, two young girls smiling arm in arm in summer dresses, a middle-aged man, his mouth open, roaring from the page with righteous indignation. Underneath it said: 'Outraged father of the two girls in the case of Jonathan Pickup, well-known restaurateur, spoke with our reporter in his suburban home today. Angry that the case against Pickup had been dropped, he said: "The man should be locked up. He's no better than a filthy animal. Young innocent girls should be protected from the likes of him. He must have drugged them or something to get them to do those things in the photographs. I won't rest until justice has been done. It's too late for my girls, but I'm thinking of others. All they wanted was to make a bit more money waitressing in the holidays and look what's happened. It's a bloody disgrace, and if the police aren't prepared to do anything about it, then it's up to us ordinary decent citizens to deal with the likes of him."' There was a lot more. Until now the details had not been publicly known, but now they were, and Jonathan had fled, although the police had decided not to prosecute.

I looked along his bookshelves and took out any interesting-looking books I could see. I carried them into his bedroom and piled them on his bed. I opened his wardrobe door and removed a pair of rich-looking dark leather boots and a thick natural-wool cable-stitched jumper, and put them on the bed with the books. Behind the kitchen door was a canvas hold-all hanging on a hook. I carried it through to the bedroom and put the books, the boots and the jumper into it, adding two bottles of red wine and one of white that were left on the kitchen shelf. Then, thinking such wanton waste of good food wicked, I went back into the kitchen and collected a dozen deserted eggs and some cold cooked sausages in a brown paper bag. I hoped Ben would like the boots and jumper—that they would fit him and that he would be pleased with me for bringing them to him.

I took a last sentimental look around the flat. Wishing to leave it all neat and tidy, I straightened the crumpled bed and plumped up the pillows. My hand closed on the handle of a leather whip—quite a small one, the plaited leather handle not more than six inches long, but the thongs, the regulation nine, much longer. They curled nastily inwards as I whisked them through the air. I wound them neatly round the handle and put the whip into the bag, taking care not to break the eggs. Everything has its uses. I picked up the bag, now unpleasantly heavy, and left.

*

I walked back through the town to the Museum and Art Gallery, down the main shopping block, through the square with the fountain and up the stone steps to the main entrance. The building was in two parts, the museum on the left, the art collection on the right, the two joined by a large foyer complete with potted plants in large plastic tubs, a cloakroom, toilets and a small shop selling postcards and souvenirs. I left my canvas bag in the cloakroom and turned into the public rooms of the art gallery.

The paintings blazed bright and brazen, along

the walls of the ground-floor gallery. I stood looking down the length of the room. They shone forth like windows looking out on landscapes full of rare surrealistic vegetation—rich, glittering acrylic jewels.

I walked to the first picture. A lagoon shimmered: blues, greens, yellows and edges of violet. Lily pads floated on the surface. A tall waterbird picked its way fastidiously across the thickly textured paint solidity. The wavering figure of a pale white girl with straw hair was reflected on the waters, wading into them. My toes curled inside my shoes, feeling sympathetic terror at unknown slimy things wriggling buried in the mud—hidden nastinesses, waiting to be disturbed, waiting to attack that perfectly smooth white body, tearing lumps from it, staining the pretty water crimson.

I escaped to the next picture. And to the next. And so round the room. Each held one of these vulnerable white bodies—a soft centre exposed in its beautiful landscape beneath the flawless blue skies. Like shell-less crabs they were, edging their way cautiously through Eden to destruction—sideways, through one picture and into the next.

I turned to leave, bracing myself to cover that vast yardage of polished wood-block floor. I felt exposed. Something might jump out of its frame and grab me, and I would join those poor soft white slugs in their alien country in the sunshine.

There was a new painting. Large Aboriginal figures stood staring out from a background of native grave-posts and ritual totems. Somewhere, out beyond the tightly knit group and the grave-post barricade, the landscape burned and glowed. In its place, in proportion. There was a message in all this somewhere, but today was not the day to get it. I made it to the door.

I collected my bag from the cloakroom and walked out into the cheerful, never-ending sunshine with a head full of foreboding. I walked into the square with the fountain, sat on one of the wooden seats and ate the cold sausages.

It seemed simplest to go home. I caught the bus, intending to go straight round to collect Angelica, but changed my mind. I had to get rid of the heavy bag first. I got off the bus a stop earlier and walked down the road towards my house.

The street was quiet, and it felt like three o'clock. All the women were down at the beach, except me and my neighbour. I could see her crouching on her lawn staring at one of the bald patches. She looked up as I approached and waved cheerfully.

'Gooday. Back early, aren't you?'

'Yes, I am. I didn't feel well. So I came home.'

'Shame, that. Anything I can do?'

'No, thanks. I think I'll just go inside and lie down for a bit.' As I said it, I started to feel sick.

'Yes, you do that. It's the heat getting you down, I expect. Been doing a bit of shopping by the looks of it.' She looked at the bag. 'Bit hot to be lugging heavy stuff about.'

'Yes, it is.' Pains were shooting up my arm. I dropped the bag and ran into the house. I just made it to the bathroom to be sick; the shaking and sweating subsided. Maybe it was the sausages. I washed my face and cleaned my teeth and went back outside to pick up the bag. My neighbour was standing guard over it.

'You poor thing. You do look terrible. Now you just get along in out of this heat. I'll give you a hand in with this bag.'

Feeling too weak to protest, I led her through the squeaking door and into the sitting room. 'This is really very kind of you. Just leave it in here. It's full of books. I'll put them on the shelves later.'

'Books, is it? Feels more like a ton of bricks, I must say.'

'Yes, they are rather heavy. Sorry about that. Well, I think I'd better go and lie down for a bit.'

'You do that, dear. I'll see myself out. That's if you're sure there's nothing else I can do for you.' She was looking intently round the room. 'Do a lot of reading, I see. I haven't got the time meself. Always on the go, I can tell you. Well, I'll be seeing you, pet. Just sing out if there's any little thing you need.' She left.

I went into the bedroom and closed the blinds. I lay on the bed in the gloomy heat of the endless afternoon, wondering what time had been used for before my loss of resources, congratulating myself on my withering friendships. The day after next was Thursday. By not looking past that, I started to feel better. I got up and unpacked the bag. The whip was a problem, and I chucked it under the bed. It could stay there for years, slowly buried in drifts of curly white dust; no questions asked. The boots and jumper I left in the bag ready for Thursday. I shoved them down behind a pile of old magazines in the bottom of the wardrobe, in case James saw it and wanted to keep the things for himself. Then I went round to collect Angelica.

I must still have looked ill, for Mother-in-law ushered me in, sat me down with a cup of tea, stood over me and said: 'You should get out in the fresh air more. It's not good for you to sit in that house all day. Why don't you take Angelica down to the beach in the afternoons? She loves it so, and it would do you both the world of good. You might make friends. They're an awfully nice crowd of girls. It's rather a shame, don't you think, when you have such a beautiful beach so near at hand, not to use it?'

'I do go to the beach. But I don't like it when it's crowded.'

'But you really should try to get out and make friends, my dear. Such nice girls. And they all have tiny babies, bless them, so you would have such a lot in common.'

'Well, perhaps I will. I'll go down one afternoon soon.'

'That's good, my dear. I only want to see you happy, you know. And James. It worries me to see you brooding by yourself all the time.'

'I do go out, you know. I've been out today. And I'm going out on Thursday. I do have friends of my own.' I decided not to tell her about Jonathan. I also decided, at that moment, not to give Tuesdays up. I would go up to town anyway.

'Yes, I know that, my dear.' She sat down opposite me in a large floral-covered armchair. 'But perhaps it would be better for you to make new friends round here. With girls you have something in common with. Circumstances do change, you know.'

The phone rang, which was most convenient. I felt sick again. When she came back into the room I said that I had to go. She stood on her moody concrete and waved us down the road. We squeaked straight down to the beach in search of fresh air to do me good. A few of the older children were whooping over the sand and playing on the swing. I lifted Angelica and carried her in my arms along the edge of the water. She wove her fingers into my hair and breathed her soft rabbit-breaths into my ear. We stood a long time staring into the waves. The shrieks of the chasing children sounded echoing and empty across the darkening beach. As the darkness deepened, they slunk home in quiet huddles. The narrow strip of depleted scrub and bush grew black—an even, deep black. At the far end of the beach away from the suburb, the bush was thicker and stretched away unbroken, racing away from the houses, gaining strength as the gap widened, building up like a breaking wave, in a thick foaming black line against the darkening sky. I snuggled Angelica's damp warmth against me. As I watched, two tall black shapes peeled away from the wall of blackness. They flitted from the shadows and picked their way over the rocks at the end of the beach down on to the sand. Long slivers of black. Each figure held a long, tapering spear poised at shoulder height. A flashlight clicked on. Murmuring voices drifted on the air. They were local men out fishing for flounder. Each wore long wading boots. Each carried a powerful torch to transfix the flat fish in a circle of light on the sandy shallow sea bottom. They carried spears with which to stick them. They came on in stealth and silence, their lights moving slowly through the shallows towards us. We turned and walked back to the pram. I tucked Angelica in and squeaked off up the road. The house was dark and uninviting. But there was nowhere else to go. We were home. Angelica had gone to sleep and I didn't wake her. She would wake in the night to be fed. No matter. It helped pass the time.

*

Wednesday drifted by. I mooned, preoccupied about the house, and watched my neighbour through the slats of the blind. She was scattering little grey pellets on the bald bits.

I read the books I had taken from Jonathan's. There was nothing about his disappearance in the daily paper. I supposed it was of little general interest.

In the evening James phoned.

'How are you, love?'

'I'm fine thank you, James. How are you?' It was hard to form words after a speechless day. I didn't talk much to Angelica. She would probably grow up deprived.

'I'm fine too, darling. Tired, of course. Been bloody busy. Sorry not to have phoned before. I didn't get a chance until late last night and then I was scared I'd wake you or something. Listen, darling, I know it's a drag, but it doesn't look as if I'll get home again tonight. We're still flat out finishing off a bit of film we need tomorrow. Tomorrow I'll try to be home at a reasonable hour. All right?'

'All right. But you know I won't be home till late. It's Thursday tomorrow. Couldn't you come home this evening instead, and work tomorrow? It would be so nice.'

'I'm sorry, darling, but I've made all my arrangements now. Besides, I told you I've got to have this film ready for tomorrow. Can't you cancel Thursday? I mean, it's only one of many. There's always next week. If you can put it off that long, that is.'

'I'm sorry, James. They're expecting me, you see. I couldn't let them know in time.'

'No, I suppose not. Never mind. At least we'll see each other for a bit tomorrow night. And we'll have a lovely weekend, I promise you. We might borrow the car and go for a picnic. I could use a bit of fresh air and a day away from all this carry-on. What do you say? Would you like that?'

'Yes, James. That will be lovely.'

We played our word games for a little longer, told each other that we loved us, and hung up.

I could safely begin anticipating tomorrow—but not quite. As I sat in the dark on the floor by the phone, a scrambling began at the fly-wire door.

'Hello in there,' came the voice of my neighbour. 'Are you home?' She paused. 'Only—if you are—I've something to show you. If you can spare the time.'

Was she being sarcastic?

She entered the room. The light clicked on and I rolled sideways on the carpet, covering my eyes.

'Whatever's up, pet?' she enquired, prodding me with her hush-puppied foot. 'Not still feeling crook, are you?'

I sat up and assured her of my excellent health.

'Oh well, that's all right then,' she said. 'Now tell me, what do you think of this?' She waved a glossy booklet in front of my face.

I took it from her and flicked through it. A line of little gnomes danced before my eyes, performing a series of tiny gnomic steps. They stood up, sat down, spun round—a whirling chorus line in little green breeches and bright red hats.

'You're not looking at it properly,' accused my neighbour. 'You're going too fast to take it in.'

I flattened the booklet out on the floor and we

went through it together while she explained her plan.

'It's for those bits where the grass hasn't taken right,' she told me, as we paused to admire a wrought-iron lace-work Spanish-colonial-style bird table. 'I thought that if I put a few pieces of garden furniture over them and maybe one or two of these little fellows'—her grass-stained forefinger stabbed a passing gnome—'the whole effect would be better.'

I agreed with this, but she wasn't listening. Her mind was racing on, anticipating problems. 'Of course,' she said, 'it won't be that easy, you know. All that dust off the road. I'll have to be out there dusting quite a bit, I can see that. All work and no play, that's me.'

I smiled encouragingly and she prepared to leave.

'Well, that's that, then,' she said. 'I'll get off home now and fill in the order form straight away.'

I saw her to the door, which creaked shut behind her. Her voice drifted back through the darkness.

'That door could use a spot of oil, dear. I'd get hubby on to that right away, if I was you. Goodnight then.'

'Goodnight,' I said and went inside to bed, falling straight to sleep.

✳

It was dark when my heartbeats woke me, thumping in my ears; and I lay very quiet while the drumming subsided. Feeling cold, I stretched over the edge of the bed and groped underneath for a nightdress. I dragged it out, shook it free of dust and put it on. I went into Angelica's room and stood over her, listening to her breathing, trying to match her light rapid breaths with my own. This had been a habit from her birth. I had waited then, half in agony, half in hope, for the breathing sound to stop. Angelica showed no sign of waking, so I went back to bed; but before going off to sleep, I got up again and dragged the big bag from the wardrobe. I crawled under the bed, found the whip and put it into the bag with the boots and jumper. I returned to bed and lay sleepless, waiting for Thursday to start.

*

It started badly. Mother-in-law said she had a cold.

'Not a bad one. Just a sniffle, really. But I'm wondering if we should risk Angelica's catching it.'

'Oh no. Look, don't worry. Really there's no need. She's very tough.' I shook her up and down to prove she had no rattles or loose parts. I hadn't the faintest idea how tough she was. Angelica had never been ill. Her face shone, pinkly trusting, up at me.

'Well, I don't know, my dear. A cold can be a very nasty thing for a little baby. I'm not sure I should be with her today.'

'Well, perhaps it will be all right if you don't breathe on her.' I was beginning to panic. 'Just keep her at arm's length or something. I've got to go. I've got to go now because of the bus. I've got to go because I'm expected. It's too late to let them know. They're not on the phone, you see—that's the trouble.'

I pushed Angelica at her and retreated through the double windows. I kept up these disjointed justifications until I was halfway across the lawn. Then I ran. I ran up the road repeating 'I have to go', like the Little Red Engine thinking it could, but not so worthy.

The bus to town was running late and I almost missed the second. The driver was looking over his shoulder. When he saw me he gave a cosy smirk of welcome and started up. 'Gooday, as the natives say. Bit late, aintcha? Waited for you, though, didn't I?'

'Thank you very much.' I smiled and tried on a grateful expression.

'Hold very tight, please. Ding ding,' he yelled. The bus lurched out of the depot and into the oncoming traffic. The street exploded with furious car horns and blazing sun, and the black tarmac ahead danced and dazzled, liquid with heat. The transistor roared with static. I started to feel better. I felt in my bag for my purse, opened it and handed him the fare.

'No, love. Forget it. Can't charge you for it, can I?' He curled his lips and vibrated them together thoughtfully. 'I've washed me hands, see.' He waved them both at me. The bus lumbered towards the middle of the road, and the passengers gave us a collective glare. He hauled it back, half-standing in his seat, both hands heaving on the wheel. 'And I've cleaned me nails. Like you said.'

'Did I?' I looked at his hands. The tops of his nails were white and scraped-looking against the plastic steering wheel.

'Yeah. You said, "Next time clean your nails first. I'm scared I'll catch something." Well, it's next time and I have.'

'Yes, I see you have. Well, that's great. I'll see you later then.'

'Yeah. See you later. See you tonight then, eh?' This time he winked and rolled his fat top lip into a passable Presley sneer.

I walked down the centre aisle to an empty seat at the back of the bus. He was yelling something after me. 'I've got a nailfile in me pocket. In case they get dirty during the day, like. And I've got a packet of them impregnated cleaning pads from the chemist to wipe me hands with.' I smiled and waved in a feeble parody of the Queen, shoved my bag under the seat and sank down with relief.

My fellow passengers sent me brightly enquiring looks. I smiled and waved at them too, and then turned and gazed fixedly through the window at the retreating city centre. When everyone had settled down I took out my comb and dragged it through my hair. My eye caught the driver's in the mirror fixed above his seat. He sent me a cheerful wink and ran his tongue greasily round his lips. I went back to window-gazing.

The bus stopped at the large general hospital on the outskirts of town, and an old man in an almost floor-length grey raincoat got on. As he walked down the bus towards me, I saw that the raincoat was open. It covered a synthetic shirt buttoned to the neck. A string vest matted with grey sweaty chest-hairs peeped through the shiny transparent nylon. Knee-length grey shorts, varicose veins, tartan ankle-socks and plastic peep-toed sandals flashed at me intermittently as the raincoat swung open and shut.

He carried a large Gladstone bag. He settled himself into the seat opposite mine and started to cough: something rattled deep down behind his string vest. He began searching through the bag on his lap, desperately. It was clearly a race against time. The rattling was getting higher, and whatever it was down there had nearly reached the surface. A red-and-blue striped pyjama jacket landed limply in the aisle, raising grit-bursts of dust and trampled chicken feathers. The old man was throwing everything out of the bag in an effort to find something. With a sigh of relief, which collided in his throat with a sickeningly gurgling cough, he pulled out a clear plastic container. He held it up triumphantly, like a happy hostess displaying the latest line at a Tupperware party, and spat loudly into it. He fitted a lid on it, taking great care to make it airtight. Satisfied, he held it up to the window and swirled its contents round and round, watching rapturously.

'They give me the little pots at the hospital. I've got a lot more in here.'

I leant over and picked up his pyjama jacket and a squeezed-out mangled tube of toothpaste that had landed just under my seat. He took them from me and tucked them carefully away. Then he gently placed the plastic pot on top and cuddled the bag against his chest. Resting his chin on the pot, he looked over at me and said: 'What they do is, I send this stuff back to them at the hospital and they look at it under a microscope. I've got this chest infection, see. Had it for years. Don't seem to be able to shift it.' As if reminded of its tenacity, the chest rattling started up again, followed by the frantic scrambling through the bag.

The routine was repeated many times during the journey. Being nearest to him, I helped manage his possessions each time as they flew about the bus, and there was no time to gaze out of the window at the passing scene.

The bus stopped dead just as I was feeling under my seat for the old man's comb. I fell forward and banged my forehead on a box of bananas.

'There's yer dopey-looking boyfriend waiting for you. Pretty, ain't he? Here's his fan mail.' The driver waved a fistful of letters at me.

I handed the old man his comb. It was metal with wide teeth—designed to do battle with a good deal of thick hair, clearly a relic of his youth, since now he was almost bald.

'Thank you very much,' he said. 'Nice comb, this. Used to use it on me dog. When the dog died, seemed a shame to throw it out.'

'You gunna stand chatting all day then?' yelled the driver. 'Only I've got a lot of stuff to deliver, you know. People waiting on me.'

I said goodbye to the old man.

'See you tonight then, darling,' whispered the driver, as I took the letters and left the bus. As it pulled off I realised too late that I had left the boots and jumper under the seat. And the whip.

*

Ben crossed the road. I handed him his mail, and we walked arm in arm towards the house. I told him about the forgotten bag, but he said it didn't matter. It was too hot to think about jumpers and boots; he had no use for a whip right now. He didn't ask where the things had come from, and I envied his lack of curiosity.

It was a golden morning, and the fence posts were touched with it. Ben's hair blazed. The gums shed golden shadows.

There were lots of extras in the yard that I couldn't remember seeing before. Tiny bright butterflies played in a holly bush, whose tough, deep-green leaves were cracked from summer heat, each crack lined with gold dust—veins of rare richness. Fluffy, comic-book yellow baby chickens scurried resolutely in the dirt under an old iron ploughshare which was covered in sun-tinted saffron-coloured rust. The air smelt of Vicks vapour rub. I thought of something I'd been told: that every returning Australian knew he was nearing his home-land when, after days at sea with no land in sight, the eucalyptus smell drifted on the wind from the unseen coast and touched his nostrils. This morning I thought it a lovely story. Sentimental tears started in my eyes, and I sniffed to stop my nose running.

Ben heard. 'Listen, I told you it doesn't matter about those things. Things just aren't that important. Not ever.'

'It's not that. It's just so beautiful here. Specially beautiful today, somehow.'

We stood on the old wooden verandah looking over the golden yard.

'Yes, it is beautiful. Feels good. Nobody near. Lots of space to think in.'

We were standing in a cloud of strange perfume: a heavy scent. Ben said it was called patchouli—a friend had sent him a little phial of it from Sydney, and he would give me some. Prostitutes had used it during the reign of Queen Victoria, he believed. It was Indian, he said. Mystic. Oriental. Sexy.

We went into the kitchen. I sat at the large scrubbed-pine table and took off my shoes, flattening my feet on the cool grey stone floor. Ben put the kettle on the stove and a Bob Dylan record on the stereo deck in the living room, a nice sunny countryfied Dylan to go with the morning—'Country Pie'. He turned the volume up and opened the serving hatch in the dividing wall. We sat opposite each other, drank tea and smoked, feet tapping, heads nodding, mouths making silly smiles.

I was waiting for playtime, but Ben left the kitchen and returned with a block of drawing paper and a clutch of thick draughtsman's pens. He put them in a small brown rucksack.

'Come on. We're going for a walk up the valley.'

I felt my face doing various well-recorded surprised things: jaw dropping, mouth opening, eyes widening. I was wondering what I had done. Sure it was to do with last week's scene—my punishment. I had hoped for something more interesting.

Ben was filling a flask with water and putting biscuits into a paper bag. He left the room again and came back wearing one digger hat and carrying another. He jammed the second on to my head. It came down over my ears. He pulled it off and balanced it carefully on top of my hair.

'These belong to the old man. Genuine World War Two army issue. How about that? Getting any warlike vibrations?' He put his pouch of tobacco and a packet of cigarette papers into his jeans pocket, took off his shirt and picked up the rucksack. 'That's it. Get your shoes on. Let's go.'

He walked out into the yard, and I watched him through the window. He turned and beckoned me. I followed, through the yard and across the brown paddock nearest the house. He zig-zagged across it, avoiding the biggest clumps of thistles, and I followed a few yards behind. The hat was making my head hot and itchy, and I stopped to take it off. I also removed my T-shirt, which I draped over a large woody-stemmed prickle, placing the hat on top.

Once through the paddock, the way along the valley led in a stretch of boulder-strewn rough grassland round one side of a conical hill, but Ben didn't go that way. Instead he started up over the lower grassy slopes of the hill. I hurried to catch up.

'I thought you said we were going along the valley?'

'Yes. But then I thought of climbing the hill. It's great up there. High up, hot and grassy. Tucked right up under the sky. You can see for miles. Like a plasticine map. You'll see.'

We were at the edge of the strip of bush that curled round the middle section of the hill. As we entered it, the silence wrapped itself round our heads. The air was cool and fragrant, and the bush sparse. Four years before a bushfire had roared up the valley. The flames had crept up the hills on either side, scouring them clean of growth. There were groups of new, slender, dusty green saplings among the remaining large trees which bent and rustled in our ears, tickling our armpits as we pushed through them. Twigs snapped under our feet. Strips of bark layered the ground.

The growth became slightly thicker as we climbed, and we returned to single file. Large fallen tree trunks, some still blackened at the edges, made their own clearings in the bush. Most were half hollow, the wood inside a soft, damp, sawdusty, insect-riddled, rubbery pulp, the outsides covered with open-pored sponges of beige fungi and emerald-green mosses. We rested on one, sitting back to back. I sealed my skin inch by inch to his. We drank water from the flask. Ben rolled two thin cigarettes and passed one to me over his shoulder. We sat in a cloud of fragrant head-blurring smoke and admired the view. Below us, through the trees, was his neat wooden farmhouse: the paddocks, the creek, the duck pond, the yard. Beyond that was the township. A central group of simple square Georgian houses, with tiny rectangular windows and doors, stood clustered round a sandstone church—small boxes arranged round a bigger box topped by a tall narrow triangle, a geometrical study in gentle local stone. Behind the township, little fenced-in fields backed into grassland dotted with miniature cows, distant blobs on four short sticks. The grasslands climbed halfway up the rounded hills on the other side of the valley, the tops of the blue-green trees blurred smokily against the bright blue sky. High up, centred in the blueness, was the sun. Golden shafts came straight at us from its central silver disc: fine playground slides of gold. It looked just right for the sky to split and God and all His angels to come streaming down—sliding down the fat sunbeams, sandalled feet pink and kicking, white robes billowing.

Loud bird cries started up in the trees around us. Ben pinched out his cigarette and took out the block of paper and a pen. He started to draw.

'I've been thinking of doing an engraving of this nostalgic old township as seen from up here. I could sell them around the place as a stopgap. In pubs, streets—anywhere.'

'Good idea. Do you need money that badly?'

'Yes, my love, I do. My old lady doesn't earn that much. Paints and that are bloody expensive. How are you and James getting on?'

'All right, I suppose.'

'Good old James. You don't have to worry about him. Fortunately he has little of the self-destructive in his being. Or he manages to channel it.'

'I don't worry about him.'

'Glad to hear it.'

'Well, I don't.'

'It's a drag, all this worrying about people. Just another word for interference. Let's get on. I'm not in the mood for this today. I need to be by myself to think about it properly.'

'I'm sorry if I disturb you.'

'Jesus. We can do without all this fish-and-chips-for-the-lady false humility. Let's go.'

We went on.

Birds screamed up in the trees. I looked up and saw they were large and black. Dislodged bits of dry twig, and showers of shrivelled leaves, fell on our heads as the birds crashed from tree to tree. A big group of them seemed to be moving up the hill with us. The bush grew thicker. We zig-zagged to avoid the pieces of tough old growth that scraped at the bare skin above our waists.

And then we stepped out of it, onto the small area of clear rocky land at the top. The grass was short, greyish-green and springy, the rocks large, sandy-brown and warm, lying on the ground like butchers' blocks. Ben slung down the rucksack, kicked off his desert boots and unzipped his jeans, signalling that I do the same. He crossed to one of the largest stones and stood beside it naked, his arms folded across his narrow chest, his hat tilted forward to shade his eyes, chewing the leather chin strap, watching me. I undressed, crossed to the stone and lay down on it, flat on my back, staring into the sun—until he towered darkly over me in the best romantic tradition and blotted it out.

'What about the view?' I murmured.

'Fuck the view,' he murmured back, as if he were insulting it.

Sometimes I wondered, but now was not the time to question his attitudes. His chosen stone was slightly hollowed out at the centre. It set us into a curious rocking motion as we moved together on top of it. The day came and went. Little flashes of light and dark.

Time passed, well spent. The sun moved in the sky. Ben's hat fell off. Perhaps the earth moved under us. We simmered gently in our hot rock crucible, slippery with patchouli oil and sweat. We slept. Waking simultaneously, we stared into each others eyes, put our noses together, screwed our eyes back shut, opened them again at the same time and wondered at the one enormous super-eye that looked back. We unpeeled ourselves and sat up. Ben fetched the water and the bag of biscuits. He rolled us an extravagant joint to finish up the picnic. He waved the empty pouch in the direction of everything else.

'And now,' he said, 'you may look at the view. Since that's what you came for.'

I knelt up on the rock and looked at it. But not

for long. The land below bled away in a runny blur of colours. Rainbows slowly dripped at the edges of the visible world. I was trying to see through some bars that had appeared in front of my eyes. I recognised my eyelashes.

I woke up alone. It was very quiet and very hot. My jeans lay carefully folded at my feet, shoes on top, toe to toe. A roll of paper stuck out of one shoe, with a message written in back-sloping capitals: MEET YOU AT THE TREE TRUNK. HURRY UP.

I hurried to dress, scared of being alone so close to the sky in the silent heat of mid-afternoon, and raced back down the hill. I had a feeling of being watched, of being followed. As twigs snapped under my feet, so twigs snapped behind me, echoes under someone else's feet. They snapped off to one side. Then the other. I was surrounded—escorted, it seemed, off the hill. I stopped, and so did the snapping sounds. Looking up, I saw the birds—silent, dull black and dusty, watching. Narrow shapes flickered in the green light between the tree trunks. I shouted in terror and they were gone. My terror called back to me, rebounding through the trees, carrying the memory of the sinister flounder-fishermen at the beach, the pictures in the museum—the squashy white figures, the staring Aborigines. But there were no Aborigines left in this state. They were dead—the last a woman who ended life as a fashionable pet in all the better drawing rooms of Hobart Town. Alone on the hill I knew I was being watched—being willed away, by a people who no longer existed. I ran. Young growth slapped and wound itself round my arms, breasts and back in stinging tendrils. Trees grew faces and laughed, stretching out their roots as traps to trip me—the fleeing figure in a Disney wood.

I reached the log. Ben was sitting astride it, hunched over, drawing. I sat on the ground and leaned against it. It made a shield between me and the hill. I concentrated on breathing slowly. My mind cleared. My trembling ceased.

'Feeling better?' he asked.

'Yes. I got frightened up there alone. I ran down too fast.'

'Yes. I would have stayed. But you were so asleep I thought I'd come down and make a start on this. You sleep a lot, don't you? Always falling asleep. We'd better be getting back. They'll be home soon.'

I sat and waited while he packed up his things. I didn't tell him about being watched and driven from the hill.

*

Something was happening down below at his house.

Little black-and-white cars with blue lights on top were turning up the narrow dirt track that led round the side. One car stopped at the front corner and the other went on round into the back yard. Four tiny dark-blue uniformed figures got out. Two went round towards the front door, and two crossed the yard and disappeared into the shadow of the verandah.

Ben stopped. 'Jesus Christ. What's happening down there? It's the fuzz. Those are cop cars, aren't they? Oh no, not again. What've I done this time?'

As we watched, the two sets of figures came from the back and front of the house and held a meeting in the yard.

'The bastards stopped me yesterday. I came up to town last night, trying to score some stuff. Heard there was some about. A little bit of cool inspiration for sale.' He laughed. 'They stopped me in the street. Asked what I was doing in the city. Playing silly buggers. Asked me if I didn't think I was a bit young to be wandering about after dark. Didn't search me though. Lucky for me. I suppose they've come out here now to turn the place over.'

'Will they find anything?' I hoped we had smoked it all.

'No. They're not that smart. They'll never find it.

Besides there's nobody home. Can't bust their way in, can they? It's against the law. We'll just sit up here and wait till they go. Shouldn't be long, they're just having a little chat about it. The bastards hate to give up. What are they doing now?'

They were splitting up again—two round the front, two round the back. We waited. This time they didn't reappear.

'Jeez. They've gone in. They must've gone inside. The buggers have broken into my house.'

He ran, and I followed without thought, over the long-grassed lower slopes, through the large brown paddock thick with thistles, not looking where I was going, praying hard: Our Father Who Art in Heaven, don't let there be a fuss—please. My ankles turned on the hard rutted dirt of the paddock.

The prickly clump, wearing my T-shirt and the hat, flapped in the corner of my eye, an absurd scarecrow. I stopped to collect the things. There was no hurry, I thought. This was nothing to do with me. Better to wait until it was sorted out. The police needn't know I was here. If they did, they would only ask questions—perhaps start watching me, making life difficult. So I waited, sitting in the paddock under a little cloud of tiny sticky flies, until the sound of slamming car doors reached me.

I walked slowly back to the house and went round the back. It was quiet. The chickens had fled.

I entered the kitchen. Just inside the door a vase of dried grasses was lying smashed on the flagstones. Jars of herbs had been emptied out on to the floor; their fragrance hung in the air. The old Chinese tea canister had been upended on the table, and as I watched, it slowly rolled to the edge and clattered to the floor. I walked over to pick it up. Bright orange dried lentils scrunched noisily underfoot. I noticed that the red-and-gold lacquer on the tea canister was badly scratched. I found the lid and put it back on the shelf. Shredded cigarettes clogged the sink. Every container in the kitchen had been emptied. The contents of a box of soap powder lay over everything, an unseasonal snow. There wasn't a sound. I was too scared to call out, thinking of death. I saw his body lying tangled in a heap of bright old clothes, his tall lizard-skin boots standing empty nearby. A blaze of distorted sound flared through the serving hatch. It adjusted itself, the volume settling down to an electronic roar. Not sunny. Not nice.

Do you, Mr Jones?

The cracked voice crept and threatened round the walls, sliming them with menace. I went into the room. Records and books were thrown everywhere. Beautiful cushions had been cut to pieces; their creamy stuffing made earthbound clouds on the floor. He was sitting on the rug in front of the large empty fireplace, curled over, his arms cuddling his knees. I sat beside him. He lifted his face. A purpling knuckle graze spread from the corner of his mouth up over his left cheekbone. Tiny horseshoe-shaped tooth marks welled with scarlet along his lower lip. His nose ran, and he wiped it on the back of his hand. He sniffed and spoke. He said they had taken some dried basil away in a plastic bag. It was going to the laboratory to be analysed. They were sure when they found it that they'd got him this time. He started to laugh, making his lip bleed. Bright blood clung in thick strands across his teeth as his lips drew back in laughter. I said I was sorry this had happened. He asked what it had to do with me. He was worried about the effect it would have on his wife. As he spoke, the old blue station wagon pulled up outside.

*

I stood at the window as Gloria walked round, neat in her school-teacher clothes, to the child's side of the car. She opened the door, and the boy climbed out clutching a spilling armful of his bright school paintings. They turned hand in hand towards the house. Seeing me through the window, they smiled and waved. I ran to the back door to try to tell them what had happened before they walked in and found it. I met her. The boy was dawdling behind, searching under the bushes for the chickens, calling to them to come to him, his paintings falling forgotten in the dust.

'The police have been here,' I said. 'They were searching for drugs. They found nothing, but they made a mess looking. We'll clear it up quickly. It won't take long.'

I ushered her in like a guest. She walked across to the table and stood trickling handfuls of spilt tea through her fingers as she looked round the kitchen. The boy came in. He said nothing, but started a kind of flat-footed shuffle over the crunchy mess on the floor, enjoying the noise it made under his shoes, swaying to the music from the next room.

'Is he here?'

'He's next door.'

She went out. The boy and I stood staring at each other. The record stopped. The needle scratched loudly across its surface.

'Ouch,' said the boy. 'Daddy gets cross if I do that.'

Angry voices were coming through the hatch. I shut it. The boy sat, head bent, at the table, tracing patterns in the tea leaves with his finger. He said he was hungry. I got him a glass of milk and picked some untrampled biscuits up from the floor for him. When he had finished I asked him where the broom was kept. We fetched it together. I swept everything on the floor into a heap while he cleared the table, carefully adding his small hands of tea-leaves to the debris on the floor—he frowned with concentration, as if constructing a house of cards. We swept everything into a cardboard box and carried it out to the incinerator.

We came back inside—someone was crying in the next room. I put all the empty jars and containers back in their places and the boy ran the water hard to unclog the sink. He didn't ask why the place was in such a mess. We were just finishing, and I was wondering what to do with him now when there was a loud crash of breaking glass from the next room. The child shrieked in fright and ran towards the sound. He was wearing long grey socks, with narrow blue bands round the tops, and incredibly English-looking brown leather sandals. The backs of his knees looked golden-brown and very vulnerable. That is what I thought. I stood in the kitchen thinking it over and over, until outside the station wagon started up. 'Daddy's gone, daddy's gone,' wailed the child from the next room. I went in.

They were both standing gazing through the

shattered window. She turned to me.

'He's gone to see his sister. To tell her how awful, how bourgeois we all are, I suppose. It's a shame he had to leave through the window.' The child's wails became louder. She picked him up, told him not to mind. 'Daddy will be back. You'll see.'

'When will he come back?'

'I don't know when exactly. But he will come. Perhaps tomorrow. He'll probably sleep at Aunty's tonight.'

She dropped him still sobbing into a chair and searched through the records on the floor, picking one up and putting it on. It was a child's record with stories and music. A cheerful song about a pirate with a wooden leg who sailed on the deep blue sea filled the room. The child stood next to it, chewing his thumb, still sniffing. After listening for a minute or two, he shuffled off to his room, returning with scissors and a pile of old magazines to cut up.

'Somebody's been in my room too. It's all messed up. The bed's all thrown on the floor. Has someone been sleeping in it today?'

'You sound like the three bears,' said his mother. They both laughed.

'Who's been sleeping in my bed?' he shouted, deep-voiced as any father bear.

'Now you stay here and we'll fix everything up nicely again.' As she spoke she started putting the records back in their sleeves, not looking to see which record belonged in which cover. I gathered up the ruined cushions and carried them outside to join the cardboard box. The room was quickly made tidy again—neat and empty—but the broken window remained. It was important to fix it. Hot days. Cold nights.

Gloria went into her husband's workroom and came back with a large strip of unprimed canvas.

'He won't like us doing this. Serves him right. There's a horrible mess in there. Lots of drawings torn up for some reason. I'd better not touch anything. He must be feeling bad about it, but it's his own fault. He didn't say where he was going last night but it was pretty obvious. I said there would be trouble. He said he didn't care. But he cares now all right.'

I felt close to her and happy. I saw him as a ridiculous figure, capering off somewhere, on the horizon.

We nailed the canvas over the window area. The late afternoon sun filtered through, and the room became pale as oatmeal. Next we went into the bedroom. Two mattresses lay on the floor. Unsuccessful efforts had been made to rip one open. The loose floorboards had been taken up, exposing Ben's old clothes collection. Gloria sat pulling them out. She picked up a *crêpe de Chine* dress, covered in a seed-packet print of sweet peas in bloom—one of his favourites, his World War Two tart's dress: we had invented street lamps for him to stand under in it, singing the chorus of 'Lili Marlene'. She held it against herself and strutted across the room. She pirouetted, waved a grotesquely limp wrist and shrieked 'Bloody hell. What next? My husband the transvestite. Look at all this stuff.'

She scrabbled among it. Stray garments wheeled over her shoulder and draped themselves over the furniture. 'Look at this. It's unbelievable. Where did he get all this stuff from? He's mad. Everyone's right. He's bloody mad.'

She rushed over to her clothes chest. She jerked open the lid. She put back her head and wailed. 'He's been interfering with my clothes. He's been in here making them all crumpled and dirty. Look at the marks on this.' She waved the old pink velour at me like an overambitious matador. 'I'll never get them out. It's all spoilt.'

She wept. She swore. She hammered the wall with her fists. She thought of her son nearby and stopped. She gathered an armful of things and ran through the house with them, out to the incinerator. I collected those that remained. We fed the bright things to the flames and stood side by side in sisterly concern and watched them burn. I left her, standing still and tearstained, the chief mourner at the cremation. Back in the house I finished clearing up. The boy helped me with his room. Patiently he pinned back the pictures that had been torn from his wall and returned his books to the shelf, singing and talking to himself all the time. I put his bed back together and made it. Underneath it I found his teddy bear, decapitated in a pool of stuffing. He didn't notice as I held it behind my back, edged over to the window, and threw it out, praying that he wouldn't miss it until I was gone. Together we went out to fetch his mother. She prepared a meal, which we all ate together at the kitchen table. The child grew tired. He whined throughout the meal at the lack of salt. His mother took him to his bed. He took a long time to settle down, calling her back over and over to read him just one more story, to kiss him, to tuck him up. Finally he slept and his mother and I sat on the rug in front of the fireplace.

She apologised that there was no coffee to drink. 'Ben doesn't like it. He says it's bad for you. I keep a jar of it in the staff room at school. It's the first thing I do each morning when I get there, make a cup of coffee. Such bliss. One of life's little pleasures.' She laughed.

She asked me if I had to leave that night when the bus came by, saying that if I was there she wouldn't have to think about things seriously until tomorrow. I wondered what things. I said it was all right, that I didn't have to go, that I didn't want to go.

We found wood in a shed and built a fire. Putting out the lights, we sat in front of it, glowing redly at each other. There seemed nothing to say. Pieces of wood expanded and popped softly. It was getting much too hot. She spoke and grew pale. Did I know, she asked, that when a body was cremated in India, its relatives stood in silence round the flames, waiting to hear a loud pop. When it came, they clapped and cheered and gave thanks, because the small explosion meant that the dead person's spirit had burst through the skull and was free of the body at last. I said that I hadn't heard of it, but that India was a country I'd often felt I should like to visit. As I was thinking of all the weird things I had heard about India, she said 'I know what it feels like. Often I can feel something tapping about in my head. I think it's my spirit lurking round my skull looking for a weak spot to get out through.'

I supposed she was joking, but she looked very serious. She said that the doctor called it migraine, but she knew the cause, if not the name. She said she also knew the cure.

I didn't ask her what it was, because James had appeared in the doorway. I was used to James's comings and goings being announced by a fanfare of squeaks and banging doors, like those of a giant mouse, if not a rat. I blinked, expecting him to vanish. Instead he said hello and smiled very nicely. I said hello back and started to laugh, suddenly realising that he must have left the car on the road and crept round the house to catch us out. Gloria looked on in astonishment as I snorted and rocked about beside her on the rug. She saw James and fluttered her fingers up at him in what I considered an arch and irritating way. She had picked up a lot of these annoying mannerisms while she was away. I supposed that that was what was meant by travel broadening the mind. Meanwhile James hovered in the doorway clutching a new bottle of whisky wrapped in green tissue paper.

'Sorry to barge in on you like this, girls. Didn't know it was ladies' night. I thought Ben might be about. There's something I want to say to him.'

It seemed best not to enquire what. 'Well, he's not. He's gone out. To see his sister. So you've wasted your time—come all this way for nothing.'

'Not really. I'll run you home if you're ready. Mum's pretty wild with you. She says you ran out on her this morning when she told you she wasn't well. She reckoned I should come and fetch you back.'

I ignored this. 'Well, I'm not ready to leave just

yet,' I said. 'Anyway, Gloria's got a headache, and she could do with a drink. Couldn't you, love?' Gloria didn't reply but sat cross-legged peering into the fire.

I rose and went through to the kitchen. James followed me out and stood in the doorway, watching as I stretched to get glasses from the cupboard. As I turned to leave the room, he slowly rearranged himself so that he blocked the doorway. This obscurely threatening behaviour surprised me. Mild-mannered reporter Clark Kent was changing into his Superman gear before my very eyes.

'Better get back to Gloria then, hadn't we? Give the married ladies a little drinkie.'

His voice was deep and funny, and I wondered whether he'd been drinking, and tried to decide whether I minded or not. On balance I felt grateful to him for sparing me a boring evening listening to Gloria.

He took the glasses and led me back to the sitting room. Playing gentleman, he stepped back to let me through first. As I knew he would, he ran his hand over me as I passed, patting me like butter, as if he were trying to remould me. I stamped down on his lovingly polished boot and sat back by the fire, dumbfounded by anger and other emotions I thought quite excessive in the circumstances.

'You spend an awful lot of time on the floor,' he

observed to nobody in particular.

He stood over us, smiling sweetly down on our heads. He lined up the glasses on the mantelpiece, opened the whisky, poured, and handed the glasses round. He took out a squashed soft pack of cigarettes from his shirt pocket and gave us each one. He then patted himself lovingly all over to locate his matches and failing to find any collected up our cigarettes again and lit each one himself with a glowing stick from the fire. As I smoked mine, I could taste his mouth and grew moist with sexual memory. He watched me, making foxy smiles as I fell for his corny tricks. He rubbed his hands together, a nasty rasping sound, and sat down between us on the rug.

'Well now, girls, you just carry on. I've always wanted to be the fly on the wall at a real live hen night.'

I looked at Gloria. She sat unhelpfully still, her drink between her palms, the cigarette burned down between two fingers. A thin trace-line of smoke curled round the glass.

'There's nothing wrong, is there?' he asked. 'I see the window's broken. What happened?'

'The kid kicked a ball through it,' I said, not wanting to give away anyone else's secrets. Or my own.

'Did he now, the little bugger. Boys still will be boys then, eh?' he laughed approvingly. Still she didn't speak. He asked her if she was all right. Then he asked me.

'Yes, she's OK. Just tired. She had a heavy day at school. You know how it is.'

'I know how she feels,' he said, topping up my drink. He refilled his own glass and touched it against mine with a soft clunk. 'Cheers, then,' he whispered. It was romantic. Not like being married at all. I didn't say so to James, lest he accuse me of being childish.

We talked of lots of things, murmuring so as not to disturb the other woman's thoughts. He was amusing. I wondered at how I had misjudged him. We chatted, whisky-witty, down the length of the bottle. Outside, the bus came. It stopped in the road near the house. I shushed him. The driver was revving the engine, making it roar.

'You are listening to the mating call of a bus,' I told him softly.

'Like that, is it?' he whispered back. 'Confession time at last?' Shattering horn blasts followed. The engine was switched off. 'Sounds like that old bus is waiting out there for something. Seems like he ain't shifting out of there till he gets what he came for,' he said, using his John Wayne drawl.

I stopped his mouth with my hand, scared that the driver might come up to the house. James softly chewed my fingers as I sat listening. To my relief, the bus started up and drew away. The engine note slowly tapered to nothing. In my silence I heard Gloria's soft regular breathing, mixed with the slurping noise James made as he sucked at my fingers. Gloria had gone to sleep, curled on her side in front of the fire. The untouched drink was carefully placed beside her on the stones of the hearth. I crawled over to her. One of her cheeks was bright red from the fire, and I touched the hot skin with the back of my hand.

'Take your shirt off and chuck it over,' I told him.

He did so, bringing it across to us. I tucked it against her face, shielding it from the glare. She didn't wake. James knelt nearby, watching as I smoothed strands of her sweaty hair away from her high forehead.

'What a pretty sight,' he murmured and held out his arms. I went into them and cuddled close, sucking softly at the places where his neck and shoulders joined. I looked to see if I was raising the little pink pin marks on his skin.

'Little sucker fish,' he breathed, lifting the hair from my head in handfuls and licking round my ears like a mother cat. 'Come to bed with me.'

It was impossible to break off into the separate cold. 'I can't. Never get there. Let's stay here.' I mouthed my words against his skin, my tongue tapping out my morse code.

'Supposing she wakes up. Won't you mind?'

His skin was softening like pulp under my lips. I dragged my mouth across his chest. Fine silky chest hairs trailed in the moisture inside my lower lip. I caught one between my front teeth and jerked it out. He sucked in his breath and drew back, filling my ears with sea roar. He put one hand on each side of my head and held it tight, pressed his mouth on mine and spoke into it. His voice came out from my own mouth, echoing up into my head.

'Yes, we'll stay here. Don't change your mind. You're too late.'

We moved in silence on the floor. Zips peeled open softly. His hands no longer rasped, they glided with his usual stunning attention to detail—all the correct buttons pressed. He put his hand over my mouth to shut me up. At last I relaxed under him and he let me breathe. 'OK?' he mumbled. 'Was it OK?'

I wondered why he was stopping to chat. Perhaps he really had had a hard day. I assured him everything was OK. I asked him how it was for him, to be polite.

'Great, really great. Hang on a minute and I'll show you.' He seemed to be gritting his teeth. They grinned down at me, gleaming in the firelight. Superman swooped down through the darkness.

Afterwards we lay silent and nervous as our left-over heavy breaths shuffled slowly round the walls looking for a way out. I hoped we hadn't woken Gloria up. I counted slowly twice to ten, pulled myself away and sat up. I turned to look at her. She lay in the same position, her breathing soft and regular. I watched her carefully for a moment, feeling I couldn't be sure that she wasn't awake and pretending. Then I knew that I would never know and that it didn't matter. I turned back to James. He was stretched out on his back, hands neatly folded on his chest, his feet side by side pointing skywards—the dear dead knight on the marble tomb. I leant over him and put my face between him and the ceiling.

He smiled. 'What's happening?'

'Nothing's happening. She's asleep and I want to go home.' I wanted to go home very much. To curl up forever in some great dark soft bed with him. The room was grey and chilly. I wanted to sleep and forget it. I thought of what Gloria had said about not wanting to think. Being asleep would stop her doing that, so she wouldn't need me.

James groaned and sat up on his elbow, looking suspiciously about him for some trap or other. 'I suppose you're right. We'd better be making a move. I'll feel terrible in the morning. Won't be fit for anything,' he complained. As if the whole thing were my fault, as if I'd sneaked up and drained off all his vital fluids on purpose or something.

He groaned again and got onto his knees. 'Well, if we're going we might as well go,' he moaned. 'I could use a cup of coffee, though. Wake me up for the drive.'

'There is no coffee,' I told him.

'Well, tea then. It doesn't matter what it is. I just fancy a hot drink.'

'There's no tea either. It got spilt.'

'Well, hot milk then. I'll go and make some.' He staggered up and started rummaging through his clothes.

He tugged vigorously at his underpants, trying to untangle them from his trousers, and hopped idiotically round the room trying to get them on. I felt sure he would wake Gloria and I hissed at him to be quiet. Gloria slumbered. Perhaps she was afraid to open her eyes.

The fire was almost out. The room looked different, empty and sad. I felt I wouldn't come here again.

Gloria stirred and groaned; she turned over onto her side and shivered. The room was cooling. I dressed quickly and went into her bedroom, collecting a pile of blankets and two pillows from the beds. I tucked them round her, lifted her head, and put the pillows under it. The queen on the chopping block. I took one pillow away.

I decided to leave her a note.

James was dressed by now, leaning gracefully against the mantelpiece, clutching his mug of hot milk. He kicked a bit of fire-blackened wood with his foot, and it fell to ashes. The cosy little mug of milk reminded me fleetingly of Ben, rampaging alone somewhere out in the bush, scornful of such human comforts. I stared into the dying fire, lost in admiration at his courage. 'Give me freedom or give me death,' cried this phantom Ben, hurling himself at the nearest exit, not caring if it was open or shut, risking death by a thousand cuts in pursuit of a dream. I sighed, and James nudged me impatiently to get on. He skimmed the skin from the top of his milk with his little finger and flicked it into the fireplace.

'Say when you're ready,' he said.

I told him I wouldn't be long. I couldn't find pencil and paper for my note and went to look in the workroom.

I switched on the light, screwing up my eyes against the glare. Objects appeared and reappeared as if on an old flickering film-strip. A swooping grey shadow moved backwards and forwards over the room. There seemed to be some large bird trapped there, crashing through the air looking for an escape, and I crouched down, covering my head with my arms. Peeping through my fingers, I saw that the light bulb, hanging on a flex from the ceiling, was blowing about in a draught coming from a broken window above the table. I taped a piece of stiff cardboard over it and the light slowed down. The room became normal.

Gloria hadn't mentioned the broken window, but the room was a mess, as she'd said. Drawings had been ripped up. A pile lay on the table, torn exactly in half. A few had been reduced to confetti heaps, scattered, perhaps by the draught, all over the floor. Wrung-out paint tubes lay everywhere. The paintings were untouched. I looked at the one of my head, curious to see how it was. The small middle-aged woman mowing her lawn had gone from the corner. She had been painted out. Instead she was mowing away in the middle of my forehead, standing there defiantly, like a caste mark, or a visible obsession. I was surprised. We hadn't spoken of her all that much. She hadn't been mentioned at all today. This proved her lack of importance—I felt he was wrong.

'What are you doing? Hurry up.' James stood looking over my shoulder.

'Not bad is he? Interesting stuff. A bit weird, though. Could be very good, I reckon. Needs to sort himself out, though. Bloody awful mess in here. Something's been going on, whatever you say.'

I looked round the room in which Ben and I had spent so many fun-filled afternoons. There would be no more of them. Gloria's distress was too real. She had shed too much light, driven out all the fantasy with her sharp reality. There were no more interesting shadows.

James sorted through the ruined drawings. 'Here, write your note on this. Only hurry up. I need my sleep even if you don't.'

'All right. I won't be long now.' I couldn't think, with him pacing about the room making remarks. 'Why don't you go and wait for me in the car?'

He went out.

I still couldn't decide what to write to Gloria. Finally I said that James was dragging me home by the hair and I hoped everything would be all right and not to worry. I propped my note on the mantelpiece and left the room hurriedly, feeling guilty.

In the back seat of the car I went to sleep. Halfway home James stopped and made me get into the front. He was having to take the bends too slowly, he said, for fear of tipping me onto the floor—at this rate we wouldn't be home for hours. We reached his mother's house just before dawn and collected Angelica. Mother-in-law had relaxed her eternal vigil and was taking a nap. James ran ahead as I wheeled Angelica round the corner and home. He was anxious to get to bed, he said. Besides, the shrieking pram gave him a headache. By the time Angelica and I squeaked up to the door James was in bed, the sheet pulled up over his head. Clearly he was not to be disturbed.

I unloaded Angelica into her bassinet and went to the bathroom. I filled the bath with hot water and pine crystals and lay soaking and dozing until Angelica woke. Hearing her give forth a series of loud complaining hiccups, I regretfully pulled out the plug and watched the fragrant green-tinted water whirl all my sins away down the plughole. Anti-clockwise, of course.

*

James was up again and grumbling around in the bedroom. He turned out drawers looking for this and that.

I carried Angelica into the bathroom to watch her daddy shaving. I wanted to discuss the proposed picnic, if it was still on. He told me that it was. He chased a little trickle of blood down his chin with a scrap of toilet paper. Angelica smiled gummily, and James smiled back at her in the steamy mirror. He told me what to buy for the picnic at the local shop.

He said he would be back by lunchtime the next day, and that we would try to get away first thing on Sunday. He had spoken to his mother about having Angelica for the day and she was only too pleased. Everything was arranged. He was really looking forward to it, he said.

I phoned Gloria at her school. The person who answered said she wasn't there. She hadn't come in today, and the boy wasn't in his class. He supposed that one or other of them was ill, though if that was the case, it was odd she hadn't telephoned to let them know. I said that it was difficult for her, living in such a remote place, to get to a phone. He said he supposed that was it, and hung up.

As I wheeled Angelica along the narrow dusty footpath that ran beside the main road down to the small local shop and garage, I wondered what had happened, and wished I hadn't left. I decided to phone the school again on Monday. I bought everything I could think of for the weekend and wheeled Angelica back home under a covering of cans, egg cartons and cheese. Her eyes squinted through at me, slightly crossed and confiding.

*

Her Daddy was home in time for lunch the next day. He brought with him several bottles of wine and some olives from the Reffo shop near his work.

After lunch, he set about a few Saturday afternoon chores. He oiled the pram and the door. Then, since he didn't have a lawn to mow or a car to wash, he suggested we go down for a swim. I wouldn't go, not wanting to see the beach smothered under a Saturday mob.

✳

Next morning I woke and James was not in bed. It seemed very early. I could hear him in the kitchen. I went out to find him cutting sandwiches. I perched on the stool and watched him. He stuck a mug of tea in my hand.

'We're making an early start,' he said. 'So when you've got the strength, go and get dressed. I'll get Angelica ready. I've nearly finished here.' He was talking so much he cut himself.

We pushed Angelica round the corner and left her face down and dopey on his mother's bed. James took the car keys from her handbag and we left.

We drove fast down the coast road to catch a small ferry to an island just off the coast. I hadn't been there before. It was narrow, straggly, bleak, bushy and scarcely populated except for a few clusters of battered wooden holiday shacks. The beaches were long and magnificent—James was sure I would like them.

On the ferry we stood side by side looking over the rail at the water, as it churned out from under the boat in a murky froth. The day was warming. A spicy eucalyptus breeze blew in our faces. We smiled happily at each other.

It wasn't far. The ferry backed into its place. James knew the island from childhood visits and drove to a beach he remembered as being isolated and endless. It still was. We took the car as far as we could down a dirt track and staggered over sand dunes to the sea.

'When they filmed *Dr Zhivago*,' said James, 'they used millions of tons of salt to make the snow.'

'What about *Lawrence of Arabia*?' I asked. 'I wonder what they used for that.'

'Sand, I suppose,' said James.

We had reached the top of the front line of dunes. James put his finger to his lips and fell flat on his face. Wriggling forward on his stomach like an Indian, he peered over the top of the ridge, and turned and beckoned me to join him. We lay side by side looking down and along. The beach raced away into the distance on either side, its farthest limits—if they existed—out of sight, veiled in soft sea mist and flying surf spray.

'Terrific, isn't it?' said James.

'Terrific,' I said.

We whooped and hollered our way down, sliding knee-deep in sand, and falling and rolling over and over down to the beach. We swam far out beyond the breakers to where the sea was deep and blue, body-surfed back in and fell choking at the water's edges, noses, eyes and mouths streaming salt foam. We raced each other back up the beach to the soft, dry sand at the top and lay baking in the sun, wet sand sticking to our skins. As we dried out, the sand became dust-fine, leaving us with a light-golden sugar coating, like doughnuts on a bakery shelf. We lay close, pleased with ourselves. I wanted to tell him about my terror on the hill that afternoon. I tried to, and lay very still, expecting him to laugh.

But he didn't. Instead he said, 'Let's have lunch.'

'It's too early for lunch,' I said. 'We'll be starving again later on.'

'I packed plenty of things. We'll have lunch twice. Once now, and then later.' He went back to the car to get food and some ale from the Esky fridge box. He seemed a long time. I slept. He came back. He had been trying to pick up the latest cricket score on the car radio.

As we ate, James told me that there had once been

an Aboriginal settlement in this place. Aborigines had been rounded up by soldiers and a bricklayer missionary. They were put out here so as not to bother the white settlers as they seeped out across the state forming tiny townships with pretty and exotic names: Flowerdale, Baghdad, Jericho.

'They built houses for them, I think, or huts or something. Bits might well still be standing.' He tried to work out how long ago it would have been but couldn't. 'I've a vague idea of where it was, though. We could drive there and see if there are any signs of it left. It might be interesting.'

The sun was high and beginning to redden our bodies. We left the beach and drove to where James thought the reservation had been. Not far from the track we found an overgrown pile of broken pale-orange bricks. We walked round, tracing with our feet a large rectangle roughly twenty feet in length. A short way behind this, deeper in the bush, there were a few smaller squares, outlined on the ground in the same crude bricks. They were hard to see, half-buried in the soil, worn down on the surface, woven up in wiry growth. Tall trees met overhead and the sun came through in uneven blots. There were more piled heaps of smashed bricks. The fleshy weed with luminous bright pink flowers, called 'pigface', rose out of the surrounding earth, crawling over the crumbling mounds and binding the old bricks tightly together. Some other plant grew there. Bright green curly tops poked out of the ground, some in close clumps, some standing alone. Curious, I pulled at one. It came out quite easily. A poor, water-starved turnip hung on the end. I showed it to James. He cut it open. It was fibrous and woody. It kept its sharp turnip smell.

'How about that?' said James. 'They must have had some sort of a kitchen garden here and these bloody things just kept going somehow. Just kept on coming up for over a hundred years.'

That was all we could find—the wild turnips and broken bricks strewn about the ground in lines and piles. It was a silent place, damp and gloomy. A musty dead smell hung thick as mist. I had expected some-thing more dramatic: sun-warmed, ivy-covered grey stones oozing romantic history, a monument to a dead race with a souvenir shop attached. But there was nothing left. Just a small sadness and boredom.

We left to find another beach on which to have another lunch. We collected some interesting shells but threw them away when we got back to the car. Reaching the ferry in good time, we waited in a lengthening line of day-trippers impatient to return. Beer cans piled up along the roadside.

We agreed that we had had a good day.

✳

On Monday morning I phoned the school. The same man answered. Gloria and the boy were absent again. The school had still not heard. Did I, he wondered, know anything, since I kept phoning. I said I didn't, and hung up.

Next day I phoned again. No, they were still not there, but one of the teachers, who was friendly with her, planned to drive out after school to see what was happening.

I took Angelica to her grandmother's. Her cold was much better. Mother-in-law was so glad that James and I had enjoyed our picnic. She felt he looked the better for it.

✳

I caught the bus to town, and in the shiny new State Library I took out the one book there was on Tasmanian Aborigines.

On the bus going home I decided to give up Tuesdays.

There was nothing to do with them.

I collected Angelica.

Next morning I phoned the school. There was no news of Gloria; and the other teacher hadn't been able to go after all, though she planned to go today if she could get away on time. There was a lot of excitement at the school today, the man confided. Somebody had scrawled something on one of the school fences during the night. Was it obscene? No, he said, he didn't think so. Someone had written

THE TIGERS OF WRATH ARE

WISER THAN THE HORSES OF

INSTRUCTION

in white painted capitals, and signed it William Blake. The police had been called in and had spent the morning going through the school rolls. The headmaster was of the opinion that it was the work of some disgruntled parent, although he conceded that such fancy phrasing was a bit odd. Unfortunately there was no pupil at the school called Blake and records showed that there never had been. It was a puzzle he said. And a shock. The school have never suffered from any type of vandalism before. I agreed that that sort of thing could be a problem, and wished him luck with it.

On Thursday I woke early without thinking, and then remembered. James slept. He had taken to coming home in the early hours of the morning—making someone miserable, I supposed with some pleasure. I wondered if Ben expected me to come. But I didn't want to see him—only his wife. There was no sure way of seeing her alone. I would keep trying to phone her at work to arrange something. I would go out anyway. I got Angelica and myself ready to go. James slept on. He was restless, and I tried to be silent as I moved about the room. As I turned in the doorway, he moaned and waved his arms. I pulled the door shut behind me. As it was early, we went to the beach on the way. The new swing was broken; the seat had parted from the chain on one side, and it dangled earthwards. A 'Danger Keep Off' sign was propped against a leg.

I delivered Angelica and caught the bus to town.

＊

I went to the museum and the art gallery, turning left from the entrance hall. Long narrow rooms, filled with brightly lit cases of coins and manuscripts, led through to a large central room crammed with stuffed animals.

Around the sides was a series of scenes let into the wall. Stuffed native creatures froze warily behind glass windows; a moth-eaten Tasmanian tiger had pride of place, snarling dismally into eternity. On display in a corner was an Aboriginal group—the extinct people—models, not stuffed, an attractive reconstruction, as accurate as could be made, of a family group. They stood in a line on a replica beach. Behind their heads, painted sea merged into painted sky. Scattered hand-fuls of grey sand and bits of broken shells lent authenticity to the floorboards. A stuffed seagull teetered lopsidedly on a papier-mâché rock off to the side. The family smiled and smiled out upon the world. They had good teeth.

'They used to have the bones here. You used to be able to come in and look at 'em.'

The words came from behind. I turned. It was the old man from the bus.

'The bones?'

'Yeah, bones. Abo bones. Some old woman's, they was. Dug 'em up just after she died. Put 'em in a glass case, they did. Very interesting it was. Very popular. Particularly with us kids.' He chuckled and it turned into a cough, 'They're still here, you know, or so I've heard. Downstairs. In a cardboard box. You can still look at 'em, but youse've got to have a reason these days. Be a student down at the varsity or something. People are very interested in them old blacks these days, I'm told. Bit bloody late, innit?' He laughed again and choked.

We moved along together, inspecting rows of bottled spiders.

'Come and look through here,' he said, tugging on my arm.

I followed the flapping raincoat through an archway. We were in a room full of displays with moving lights. He flapped from one to another, pushing buttons and choking with pleasure as rows of multi-coloured bulbs revealed the presence of various minerals scattered across the continent.

'Not bad is it?' he wheezed. 'Not bloody bad at all. All that flaming buried treasure. If I was a younger man, I'd be off after it like a shot. Prospectin', they calls it. Prospectin'. That's it.' He looked at me. 'What are youse doing here? I'm early for me appointment at the hospital. I often come in here. Very interesting it is. Upstairs they've got all them convict things. Balls and chains and that. Instruments of torture. Would youse like a cup of tea? There's a place over the road I gener-ally go to before I goes to the hospital for me treatment.'

We drank our tea in the back of a sweet shop.

The owner had put a few tables in the space between the counters. The air had a hot sticky candy smell and was almost too thick to breathe. My hair started to cling to my head in matted fairy-floss strands.

I wondered if what the old man had said about the bones was true. He was talking again, saying that he was staying at his sister's place at present. 'While this treatment's going on. Some new thing they dreamed up. Don't know why I went home in the first place. No sooner got there than they sent me one of their flaming letters saying to come back again.' He slurped into his tea. Coloured jelly-baby scents blocked each nostril. 'Sitting drinking tea,' he suddenly shouted. 'Drinking nothing but flaming tea. Time was when things were different. Proper grog artist, I was. A regular flaming piss artist, that was me all right. Famous for it.' He gurgled into his tea, struggling for breath and sending up a fine brownish spray.

I decided to go. I stood up. 'Goodbye.'

'Goodbye then. Nice to see youse. Might see you again. I often step into the museum when I'm a bit early. Can't hang about me sister's place all day, can I? Me flaming cough frightens the bloody budgie.'

I looked back and waved from the doorway. His hand flapped back through the gloom.

On the bus I decided that Thursday could go too.

Angelica showed little pleasure at being collected so soon. She grizzled all day; and in the evening I wheeled her down the bumpy track to the doctor's surgery.

'It's just a tooth coming through. Nothing to worry about,' said the doctor.

'I hadn't thought of that,' I said. 'I'm sorry. I needn't have come.'

'That's all right. Don't hesitate. That's what we're here for,' he said, although there was only one of him. 'To set mothers' minds at rest. Especially the young ones. These things come with experience. You'll find the next one a quite different proposition. Much easier.' He smiled benignly at the now peaceful Angelica.

'There's another reason I came as well,' I said, although there hadn't been.

'And what would that be, my dear?'

I told him. That each day took too long. That I couldn't make time pass at an acceptable speed.

'I think what you are telling me is that you're depressed?'

'I suppose that's it.' He was some kind of northern English immigrant, and it was hard to follow what he said.

'Well, that's nothing to worry about, that's natural too. More common than you might think. We can help you there all right.' He wrote out a prescription and ripped it from his pad. 'These tablets will make a new woman of you, you'll see. Above all, don't worry about things. You've a fine baby there to be proud of. Don't hesitate to come and see me any time. We're here to look after you, you know. Good evening to you.'

I took the piece of paper and left. Back home I crumpled it up and pushed it into the jar on the mantelpiece.

＊

On Friday morning I called the school. From the man's tone of voice there seemed to be more excitements. Gloria was dead, he said. Suicide, it looked like. The police had been at the school this morning talking to her colleagues. Wondering why. There was no note, it seemed. She had been found by a neighbour lying still and full of broken bones under his water tower. Not quite dead.

'You're not a relative, are you?' he asked anxiously. 'Or a close friend or anything? I don't want to upset anybody.'

'No,' I replied, 'a private detective.' I dropped the phone.

＊

Next day there was a short paragraph in the paper.

James instructed his mother to say nothing of it, and it wasn't mentioned between us. I felt relieved but neglected.

An inquest was held, but in the absence of a note or any evidence of obvious intention, a verdict of death by misadventure was recorded.

Two days before the funeral Gloria's widowed mother flew over from the mainland; she wore a petalled hat with feathers on it like the Queen Mother. From the airport at the edge of town she hired a taxi to take her out to Ben's place and next morning she took the boy back with her to her exclusive Sydney suburb.

＊

On the day of the funeral it rained. That is as I remember it. There had been no rain that summer, but on this day it came. As it should. James accompanied me to the funeral; he knew his duty when he saw it. The crematorium was a square building, newly made from greasy yellow stone slabs, away from the town and standing alone on a windswept strip of high ground. It was surrounded by green well-tended lawns studded with shiny brass plaques with names and dates on. There were low walls as well, with niches let into them. You could go in one instead of into the lawn, if those who had survived you wished it, or if you had wished it yourself and written it down somewhere.

In the small shoebox chapel James and I hovered together near the back. There were few people there. The deceased's ex-colleagues huddled in a professional bunch to one side, avoiding everybody else's eye. This small congregation of strangers was standing on a carpet of slimy liverish yellow—it matched the building bricks. The coffin was there, centre-front. It was very large. I supposed that there was a lot of room left over inside it.

At the end of a brief service, the coffin lurched forward and disappeared silently through a hole in the wall—shiny purple curtains jerked together across the gap. For a time nobody moved or understood that it was over. A trickle of thin recorded organ music brought everyone to their senses. They fled the building with decent haste. Men, briefly conscious of accident and mortality, supported their women going down the outside steps. The teachers raised umbrellas stiff with disuse over each other's heads. The rain came down in neat straight grey lines.

Ben was outside. He was standing under a strangely Italianate and formal-looking evergreen tree of some kind. He stood hunched over. His hands dug deep in his jacket pockets. He wore a narrow-cut black suit, early Beatles style. The shallow velvet collar was soggy with rain. His hair was different, cut short and uneven. Water poured from his patchy head, streaming down his country-and-western singer's bootlace tie and bouncing back up in decorative fountains as it hit his shabby silver boots. People passed him by in silence, crunching over the gravel, stumbling through the downpour to their cars. James and I faced him arm in arm. James said: 'Just wait here. I'll fetch the car over.' He ran away and was lost in rain. Ben and I stood under the foreign tree and gazed at the crematorium doorway.

'Whatever happened,' I asked, 'in the time before it happened?'

'Nothing happened,' said Ben. 'Really nothing happened, a whole lot of nothing. She wouldn't speak to me, not properly. Wouldn't go out. Wouldn't go back to work. Wouldn't say why. She didn't sleep properly. I thought she should see a doctor. I told her to go, but she wouldn't. She had bad dreams at night. They were full of snow and nothingness, she said. One morning she told me there wasn't enough colour left in the world. I said that wasn't true, not if you looked properly, used your eyes. I told her I had colour running out of my ears most times, enough for both of us. She said my opinions didn't count. That everyone knew I was crazy.' He rubbed his rainy knuckles into his eyes. 'She said I drained all the colour off from her world and put it in my own. That it was all over everyone else's walls in my pictures. She said I stole bits of her life and sold it to strangers. I tried to tell her she was wrong. That it wasn't like that really. But she said I didn't understand. I didn't. I don't. She was ill really. People who kill themselves are ill really, don't you think?'

'Oh yes. I should think so.' But I didn't know.

Ben bit his nails. His teeth ground the brittle pieces. I moved a little apart from him. He spat the pieces out and spoke again.

'It was the thing with the police mostly, I suppose. My fault, no question of that. I came back next morning. I thought she'd be at work. I was going to mend the windows, clear up properly, get it all back together. But she was there. She wouldn't let me touch anything. I said I'd take the car and get glass cut, do some shopping, whatever she wanted me to do. But she wouldn't let me. Wouldn't say why. She never went back to work.

She seemed scared about it. I thought maybe she was frightened of gossip, believed someone there would have heard what had happened. It made me so angry that she should worry what that load of idiots thought about anything. I shouted at her a lot to tell me why she cared, or if she cared. I drove over there one night and wrote on the fence what I bloody thought of them. Don't suppose they got the point, though.'

'No, they probably didn't,' I said. 'Never mind, though. At least you did something. Did she mention me at all?'

'No she didn't,' said Ben. 'Not once. After the school episode I didn't try to talk to her much. She just looked after the boy and I shut myself in the workroom and got on with things. Her mother came over the other day. She spent the best part of one night screaming at me. Said I wasn't fit to be a father. She said a lot of things. Next day she upped and took the boy away with her. I didn't try and stop her. Didn't really know how. I mean, she's probably right. I've got no bread. No nothing. All I want to do is paint. It'll be better now. A nice easy life. I won't need to bother about him. He'll be better off with her. Without me. She's got bags of money—big house, all that. One more fatherless kid in the world's not going to make any difference to anything.'

James honked the car horn. He sat peering through the rain at us as we huddled under the tree.

I offered Ben a lift back to town. To his home. To anywhere he wanted to go. He refused. He didn't wish to go anywhere yet.

James started the car.

I urged Ben to phone me if there was anything I could do.

He didn't speak, and I kissed the fine line of his unmoved wet mouth.

✳

I got into the warm steamy car next to James. He put his hand on my thigh and squeezed hard.

'I'll take you to lunch,' he said.

We went to Jonathan's restaurant.

I hadn't been there since his disappearance. A new manager had been brought over from Melbourne.

A Catholic priest perched on a stool. He slid the head of a long glass of cold beer into his mouth and wiped his lips slowly with the back of his hand. We sat at the other end of the bar and drank white wine. The priest watched us for a time and then leaned toward us and said: 'You are looking so very sad. Are you in trouble?' We didn't reply. James looked embarrassed, and the priest repeated his question.

'A friend of ours has died and we have just been to the funeral,' said James. 'We are just having a drink to cheer ourselves up.'

'And some lunch,' I added.

'That's the ticket,' said the priest. 'A car crash, was it? A terrible lot of the young people get taken that way in this country, so I'm told.'

'No. It was suicide.'

'Well, God bless the poor soul anyway. Have another drink. Have it on me.'

'Actually, she was a Hindu. We burnt her. So her soul could get out of her body properly.'

'Ah well, that's a good thing then. Drink that up and have another.'

He went with us to our table. We shared a bottle of wine, and he told us he was thinking of giving up the priesthood and going into journalism. He ate no food and left when all the wine was gone.

Coming up into the street we found the rain had stopped. James returned to work. I returned home to the afternoon silence. I sat in a chair under the window and read my library book. Details lodged in my mind like grit. In following days they dug deep and irritated.

In the early hours of the day after the funeral I got up and went down through the darkness to the beach. There was no moon to see. The night sky was thick with clouds. The swing was mended. I sat on it, my toes touched the ground, and I swung slowly back and forth. The sensation was pleasant in the warm close night. The swing sighed in the air. Waves broke on the sand and withdrew, whispering quietly. The swing swung higher. A wind blew harder round my head. Sounds started in the night. Clear sharp cries blew about on the wind. One by one they were muffled under heavy sound-proofing thuds. A muted moaning shivered last of all along the dark curve of the beach.

I recognised these sounds. I now knew of the dead dramas being given a nightly run-through along the edge of the low surf. I swung high above the action as black women were pursued and clubbed to the sand by white men. Their menfolk hesitated, confused and powerless. They were killed. Bits of them hacked away. The lost pieces lay rotting for days buried under a weight of tiny carnivorous crabs. By then the women were gone; taken off in boats; tormented and tortured round campfires in nightly cabaret; put to work luring the abundant seals to their doom. The women were made to lie at the sea's edge, their brown skins glistening under sun and moon, beckoning the seals in from the deep waters of the bay with the sinuous flipper actions of their arms and the deep siren-songs in their throats. The seals swam in. They foundered, land-clumsy on the beach. The waiting men clubbed their heads to bubbling pulp, scattering crimson drops on the golden sand.

Dawn came. The show was over. The swing returned to earth.

＊

It was in the days that followed that I killed my neighbour, Mrs Olive Stacey—Ollie to her friends. Exactly when I did it is difficult to tell—I became worse at handling time. I passed my days behind the blinds. I left the house only in darkness. James came home and left again. It seemed he came more often now. Perhaps he worried about me. Perhaps he was happy at home. He bought me magazines and chocolates, sometimes tiny bottles of perfume. I lined them up on the mantelpiece. I wondered if he thought me ill. He bought me treats as though I were in a hospital—flowers sometimes. Each night when he slept I left him.

＊

During the day I stayed dreaming behind the blinds. Green dreams of the secret pulses, the unexplored places on this heart-shaped island. Lurid orange-tinged dreams of the far-off dead red heart of the continent.

'Come out, come out, wherever you are,' cackled Call-me-Ollie. She had come calling, bringing the Avon Lady with her. The coloured dreams swirled in my mind, reforming themselves in a halo round my neighbour's unsuspecting blue-rinsed head. She had come, she explained, to take me out of myself.

'What you need is cheering up,' said Ollie, 'and Edna here is just the girl to do it. Besides, pet,' she confided, 'it just doesn't do to let yourself go like this. The menfolk don't like it. Can't says I blame them either.'

The Avon Lady smiled. Her lips were slick with shiny pink grease. Her lipstick was running round her pursed-up mouth in the heat of the afternoon, making tiny rivers in the wrinkles. She beckoned me closer. Her breath smelled of dead violets. She spoke softly to me of moisturisers, indispensible in a climate so harsh to women's skins. She suggested a green cream made from cucumbers. I heard myself ordering many things, entranced by their pastel colours, the smooth plastic containers, their artificial fragrance.

Ollie looked pleased. She said she was glad to see me back on the right track. I wondered what track and where to, but it was too late to ask.

Ollie and the Avon Lady saw themselves out. The fly-wire door shut behind them, eerily silent.

*

I stayed behind the blinds. Sometimes I would part two plastic slats between two fingers and peer about.

I watched my neighbour supervise her grass. I watched the afternoon cavalcade to the beach. It kept track of passing days. James's mother called in often to see Angelica. Sometimes she took the baby out with her. One afternoon she came in with a packet of biscuits. She made us tea and sat me down for a chat. 'My dear,' she said. 'You know I don't want to interfere. But have you thought of seeing a doctor? I do so worry about you. And I know poor James does too—though he wouldn't say as much to me, of course. But I can tell.'

'I have seen the doctor, ages ago. He gave me a prescription for some tablets.'

'Oh, that's good. I'm glad you're being sensible. Are they doing you any good?'

'Well, I don't know yet. I haven't been to the

chemists to get them.'

'Why ever not, you silly girl?' She smiled kindly. 'Well, you just give me that prescription. Go and get it now. I'll go straight off and get it done. I had no idea. You only had to ask, you know. I would have got them for you gladly.'

I pulled the prescription out of the vase. Underneath it I saw the stone. I smoothed out the crumpled paper and handed it to Mother-in-law. She took it down to the chemist.

I took the tea things into the kitchen and washed them up. I went back and took the vase from the mantel-piece. The weapon fell out into my palm. It seemed familiar. I knew its shape, felt its sharp sides. Green paint still showed on the cutting edge. I put it in my pocket.

James's mother came back with the tablets and a teething ring for Angelica. She told me she hadn't been able to resist it, they made such pretty and clever things for babies these days. She fetched a glass of water and watched closely as I swallowed one tablet.

'Now don't you forget to take them,' she instructed. 'These things just don't work if you don't follow the instructions. Three times a day, it says on the bottle.'

I watched, waved and smiled as she drove away,

blowing kisses at her retreating form. Back in the house, I stood looking down at Angelica. She lay immobile on a bright rug inside her lobster-pot playpen. I wrapped my fingers tight about my stone—tight as I could stand it. I had it with me all the time. I kept the bottle in the vase.

Three times a day I tipped it out and swallowed one of the little blue pills. They left my body calm and still. My mind raced round inside it, looking for the way out. My thoughts settled down. They slowed themselves and drew far off. The scattered strands blended into a still calm voice somewhere close up under my skull. I found that I was falling asleep with James and not waking until morning.

'Surprise, surprise,' said James waking up on the first morning to find me there. He got straight up and made me tea. He let me read the paper first, whistling as he got ready for work.

Day after day I lay watching him dress. The seven dwarfs trooped in technicolour behind my eyelids as they whistled off to work. One morning, as I lay giggling to see Snow White waving them goodbye, James bent over the bed.

'Here's looking at you, kid,' he murmured, kissing me goodbye. 'I'll be early tonight. I'm getting myself better organised. Learning not to waste my time.' He tiptoed out quietly, so as not to wake Angelica. I dreamed on.

*

It was very hot, getting towards noon. Angelica fretted, neglected in her stuffy room. I felt she had used up all the air in the house, and I was driven into the open. I wanted to see the beach under the empty noon-time blaze.

My neighbour was not out front, and I had nearly passed the house when the voice came.

'Gooday, stranger. Long time no see, like they say.'

I turned to smile at her. She lugged the lawn-mower towards me through small ripples of heat. Further up, the road surface boiled and shimmered in liquid illusion.

'Just thought I'd give it a quick going over,' she said. 'Been getting a bit unruly lately.' She unwound the flex and plugged it in just inside her front door. She came back and switched it on with her foot. Above the noise she called to me: 'I'll give it a good soaking tonight. These water restrictions are very rough on us gardeners, I must say. No rain all summer. Not a drop. Everything's so brown and scorched. Gets on your nerves.'

I closed my eyes and saw the straight grey lines of rain behind my lids falling down on the funeral. I opened them again and watched the woman torturing the patch of earth. The metal blades bit into the reeling grass. My teeth ached with the whine of the mower, and the sound bounced back from every scorching surface.

My fingers curled round the stone—for comfort. Squeezing my eyes back shut, I again saw the straight lines of rain. Now they were falling on the small area of scrubby native growth I had once been able to see by looking out of the right windows. I opened my eyes. It was still there. It grew all around us, stubborn and messy, a heat-inspired trick of eyesight and anger. The stone was out of my pocket, tight in my hand, so tight it hurt. I raised my hand, opened my cut fingers and let the stone go. It turned slowly in the air and fell to the ground in front of the mower—a sudden flash and the poor dear just lay there, her little blue face gazing skywards, straight into the noonday sun.

There was a brief fuss in the street.

✳

The balance of my mind was disturbed. Not that I need bother with excuses, because nobody is going to know. They didn't suspect a crime, and they still don't.

She was killed by her own electric lawnmower—a freak accident. It had short-circuited of course; that was what they said. The smooth detective from the Hobart CID had taken the trouble to call in and tell me so, bending his knees to get himself down to my little woman's level.

'Something caught in the blades and the bloody thing blew up, pardon my French. Terrible thing to happen. Nice place you've got here—I only hope this nasty business next door hasn't upset you too much.'

He squeezed my hand reassuringly, admired my breakfast bar, and left.

My neighbours were equally sympathetic.

'She took every precaution,' they said, over and over. 'Just shows you can't be too careful.'

That's true.

Text Classics

textclassics.com.au